Hell Town

Mike Hart rode into Ranger headquarters in San Antonio, satisfied in the knowledge that he had successfully completed yet another tough chore for his masters. He had been looking forward to a well-earned break from duty, but instead was obliged to ride out again within the hour, heading north into the high plains country with instructions to locate and disable the criminals who had placed a stranglehold upon an honest community.

He went alone, undismayed by the overwhelming odds that usually accompanied his missions. Hoping to complete his assignment before winter set in, he plunged into action from the very first moment he reached Ashville, and reacted in his inimitable style.

Now he would shoot his way through the opposition the moment it reared its merciless head.

Hell Town

CORBA SUNMAN

stern

DON

ISBN 0 7090 7762 9

Robert Hale Limited
Clerkenwell House
Clerkenwell Green
London EC1R 0HT

Typeset by
Derek Doyle & Associates, Shaw Heath.
Printed and bound in Great Britain by
Antony Rowe Limited, Wiltshire

ONE

Winter was coming early to the high plains of West Texas. For more than ten days a bitterly cold wind had bored down from Alaska and all points north, chivvying cattle in open spaces, tearing at trees and chilling cowboys going about their cheerless jobs. It whistled and moaned like a herd of banshees in a helter-skelter of non-stop raids on shacks, ranches and towns all the way down from Canada, tearing at everything not nailed down, and harried the dense black-lead clouds scurrying before it like massed ships in some heavenly armada.

In San Antonio, the adobe brick office of the Texas Rangers was proof against the wind, but the loose-hinged door and windows rattled incessantly. Mesquite and scrub oak logs were burning in the stone fireplace, but did little to raise the temperature above street level. Captain Ed Buckbee sat at his rough board table, wearing a long wool overcoat, poring over a spread of maps; using a magnifying glass because the afternoon light was fading. Finally, he sighed in exasperation and got up to light a lamp.

In his fifties, his short figure running to fat, he looked nothing like the public image of a Texas Ranger. But Buckbee had gained his reputation more than thirty years before, and it had stood the test of time. He went back to the maps, frowning as he squinted brown eyes from force of habit, and had barely seated himself when the street door was thrust open and the man he most wanted to see entered the room in a blasting gust of wild tempest.

Buckbee slammed his hands down on the maps and held them in place until Mike Hart had closed the door. Hart, tall and powerfully built, wore a heavy wool overcoat and a wide-brimmed high-crowned hat. A gunbelt was buckled outside his coat, and a .45 Colt was in the open-top holster riding low on his right hip. Heavy riding boots encased his feet, and he stamped them as he approached the table.

'Mike, I've been nailed to this table three days, waiting for you to show up,' Buckbee said. 'You sure took your time coming back. I was beginning to think you were returning by way of Canada, and I told you time is running out. I need you in the high plains area west of Fort Worth before the snow flies.'

'Then maybe I'd better sprout wings and fly there.' Hart smiled, and the angular lines of his hard features softened, although his blue eyes did not change expression. Aged thirty-four, he was tough as whipcord and able to take care of himself in any situation that might arise in the life of a Texas Ranger. 'It sure looks like snow is on the way, huh? Sorry I'm late, Captain. I travelled fast as I could, but there were details to take care of before I could close that last assignment. Did you get my report? I wired it soon as I got it down on paper.'

'Yes.' Buckbee nodded impatiently. 'You did a good job, Mike, same as always. I'm glad you put a bullet through Gimp Alder. If ever an outlaw needed killing, he did. You left no loose ends down Mesquite way, huh?'

'Everything was cleaned up neat as a whistle.' Hart's blue eyes glinted as he recalled the case that had just ended. What started as a simple job of hunting down Gimp Alder, the killer, had exploded into complications that enveloped him in a bog of mysterious events which took all of his considerable abilities to unravel. But the law had prevailed under his expert handling, and although he had looked forward to a well-earned rest after that satisfactory ending, Captain Buckbee had sent him a wire urging all haste in his return to headquarters.

'I've got a lulu of a job for you now.' Buckbee smiled mirthlessly, his attention on the maps, and Hart looked closely at the pencil lines his superior had drawn. The area holding the captain's attention was in north-west Texas, and Hart felt a quickening of interest. 'We're badly stretched at this time, Mike, so I can give you no assistance beyond steering you in the right direction. I don't even have a run-down on the lawless activities that have come to my notice. All I can tell you is, a couple of the Bascombe gang have been seen around Ashville, and that ain't good.

7

You've tangled with Trace Bascombe before, huh?'

'Bascombe the bank robber,' Hart mused. 'Yeah, I grazed him with a slug but he got away by holding young Sarah Taylor hostage. She was found later with a bullet through the head.' His eyes glinted. 'I sure would like to catch up with Bascombe again. Has Ashville got a bank? From what I've heard of the place, it ain't got much of anything.'

'The Cattleman's Bank in Ashville was robbed six months ago, probably by Bascombe, but it seems he is involved in something different these days. I got a letter recently from an old friend of mine; Art Murdock owns the A Bar M ranch east of the Coulee Hills, right here.' Buckbee tapped a stubby forefinger against the map west of Ashville. 'Art says signs are that a heap of trouble is fixing to drop right into his lap. Ashville has become a hell town since Sheriff McGee was killed and the law took a back seat. Some real bad operators have muscled in, and it looks like the sky is the limit. You have to get up there soon as you can and sort it out.'

Hart's gaze was intent on the map. Buckbee regarded him, his mind running over what he knew, and he did not like his thoughts as he drew a deep breath.

'Your orders are simple, Mike, like always. You get a free hand. Talk to Art Murdock and he'll fill you in on local details. That whole area has but two big cattle spreads – Art's A Bar M and his brother Ben's Circle M. The rest of the area is small stuff – ten-cow outfits and the like. And that ain't all. Sodbusters are trying to get in there, and the cattlemen pushing west into it are nothing more than loose-rope outfits. The Murdock brothers are knee-deep in rustlers. Life for you will be anything but dull.'

'Like always,' Hart observed wryly.

'And you got to get moving pronto,' Buckbee urged. 'Pull out all the stops, Mike. You need to be on that range and in action before the snow flies. You get caught up by the weather and you'll be there all winter.'

'Is that it?' Hart swept his gaze over the map, noting features and fixing them in his mind.

'Heck, ain't that enough?' Buckbee produced a bottle of whiskey and two glasses. 'Let's drink to your success.'

'A drink?' Hart smiled. 'Is it gonna be that bad? I don't remember the last time I got a drink off you before setting out on a case.'

'Send your reports in regularly.' Buckbee smiled as he poured two drinks and handed a glass to Hart. 'Good luck.'

Hart drained his glass and set it down. He touched a forefinger to the brim of his Stetson and turned to the door.

'Be seeing you, Captain, and don't worry: I'll handle it.' He smiled and departed.

The streets of San Antonio were deserted. Night was crawling into corners and lamps had been lit. Hart looked with some regret at the nearest saloon as he swung into the saddle of his waiting black stallion and urged it into motion. He rode straight out of town, heading north, and kept moving until night overtook him. The wind tore at his big figure as he made camp in a hollow deep enough to shelter his horse and, after eating cold food, he rolled himself into his blankets and slept until dawn.

He rode north steadily over the next two weeks, following the Chisholm Trail; stopping off at ranches along the way each night for shelter and hot food. The wind never abated. Throughout the long hours of riding it attempted ceaselessly to tear him from his saddle. Low black clouds scurried overhead, and many times he expected snow before nightfall, but the sky remained devoid of moisture.

Hart rode hunched down in his heavy coat, trying to ignore the biting cold. His hat brim was pulled low over his eyes, and at times he wore his neckerchief up over his nose. His hands were protected by thin leather riding gloves, but his fingers were victims of the cold conditions, and he repeatedly banged his hands against his shoulders in a bid to encourage circulation. His eyes were never still as he pushed north, alert as a predator. He was not expecting trouble until he reached Ashville, but would not take any risks. He rode hard and fast, wanting to begin his job as soon as possible.

Late one afternoon he topped a rise in the high plains country and saw the little cow town of Ashville lying before him. It was not a township to boast about: there was only a general store, a stage office, about fifty buildings housing the inhabitants, and a couple of saloons.

Hart rode into the dusty main street, where the

late autumn wind was raising cold dust devils on the ground. Dusk was falling and everywhere looked drab and unlovely – inhospitable. The bare, wind-stripped branches of cottonwoods and scrub oak trees were flailing like ghostly arms under the force of the driving wind, and the doors and windows of the buildings rattled ceaselessly.

He spotted the livery barn at the far end of the street and rode towards it, his keen gaze missing nothing of his surroundings – and checked his horse when he spotted a lone figure standing hunched over against a tie rail in front of the bigger of the two saloons. Aware that no one in his right senses would stand outside in such weather conditions, Hart suddenly realized that the man was tied to the rail and could not move. At first he thought the man was unconscious, and then saw a slight movement.

He rode on and entered the livery barn, sighing with relief as he stepped down from his saddle. The barn was rattling and creaking under the hammer blows of the gusting wind, but the worst of the savage onslaughts was kept out by the sun-warped boards. He pushed back his Stetson, pulled his neckerchief down from his nose, and turned to take care of the black.

'You've earned a spell in here,' Hart said, patting the animal's mane. 'We've beaten the snow so far, but if we get it before we finish this chore then the ride up will be as nothing to what will come.'

'Howdy,' a harsh voice called, and Hart turned to see a tall, thin man emerging from a dusty office in the far right corner of the barn. He was well wrapped up against the cold, and appeared to be in his middle fifties. 'You look like you've come a far piece, stranger.'

'Too far on a day like this,' Hart responded.

'I'm Nat Askew. I didn't catch your name, mister.'

'I didn't give it.' Hart smiled.

'Suit yourself. Are you riding through or do you have business in these parts?'

'Right now I'm figuring on staying around for a few days. I've been chewing on that wind far too long.'

'So you came up from the south, huh?'

'You got a special interest in men riding north?' Hart asked. He paused and subjected the ostler to a penetrating gaze.

'I like to keep up with the news from down the line. Nothing much ever happens around here.'

'That ain't what I've heard.' Hart recalled Captain Buckbee's words.

'The conditions we got here are the same any place in the country.' Askew shook his head. 'I never knew this town to be lawful, even when Sheriff McGee was alive. There was always someone trying to get something for nothing, or wanting what another man has got and breaking the law trying to take it. It's a helluva note when decent folk can't live how they want because of the scum who get among them. The whole town is ailing, and needs a good dose of law to cure it.'

'The bank was robbed six months ago,' Hart said. 'Don't you call that unusual?'

Askew grinned and his taut features twisted. 'Like I was saying, that kind of thing is usual around here. They do say as how the Bascombe gang rode in and relieved us of our wealth. I was out of town that day, and missed all the excitement.'

'But it's the usual thing that happens, huh? What about the man tied to the hitching rack in front of the saloon?'

'Is he still there? Jeez! He must be stiff as a board now. Bart Crane tied him out there around noon, and said he'd shoot anyone who turned him loose.'

'Who's Bart Crane?'

'He owns the two saloons in town — tried to buy my stable last year but I wouldn't sell to him nor nobody. What would I do if I didn't have the livery and blacksmith's shop out back?'

'Who is the man tied to the rail, and why did Crane put him there?'

'That's Pete O'Hara. He rides for Ben Murdock's Circle M; came into town for supplies and fell foul of Crane, who is using him to pick a fight with Murdock, I guess. Crane reckons it'll start the war that been threatening around here, which has been simmering a long time.'

'Another of those usual things that happen in this neck of the woods, huh?' Hart nodded. 'So what Crane does around here is OK, and everybody in town is prepared to watch a man freeze to death because Crane wants it that way.'

'You can't blame folks for turning a blind eye. Crane's got a tough crew running his interests. Men have protested in the past about his activities, but they ain't breathing any more. It ain't wise to pass an opinion in this town.'

13

Hart reached into a pocket and produced a dollar. He flipped it into Askew's ready palm.

'Take care of the horse. I'll be sticking around for a couple of days at least. I'll take my rifle and bedroll and leave the saddle in your hands.'

'Sure enough. But be warned against getting involved in O'Hara's problems, stranger. You got that look in your eye which says you're interested.'

Hart slid his Winchester out of its scabbard and unfastened his bedroll from behind the cantle. He left the stable and went along to the saloon. Yellow pools of light were stabbing through the gloom that was growing in density along the street, outlining windows in the various buildings he passed. When he reached the motionless figure leaning against the tie rail he paused and drew the long-bladed hunting knife he carried in the scabbard on the back of his gunbelt. A quick slash of the knife severed the rope and Pete O'Hara fell forward on to his face in the dust.

The batwings creaked open at that moment and Hart glanced around in time to see a man darting back into the saloon. He heard an excited voice reporting his action as he slid his knife back into its scabbard, and dropped his hand to the butt of his holstered .45 to ease the weapon.

Hart crossed to the batwings, Winchester in his left hand and the bedroll across his left shoulder, and peered over the swing doors. Many lanterns were burning around the walls of the bar, and a big, pot-bellied stove was alight in the centre, throwing heat almost to the corners. There were about a dozen men inside, all of them frozen into inactivity by the report that someone had cut Pete O'Hara free. Four of them were roasting on chairs around the red-hot stove.

A bald-headed man wearing a near-white apron was behind the long bar, poised with a drying cloth and a glass in his hands. His pale eyes were filled with an expectant glitter as he gazed at Hart when the Ranger shouldered through the batwing doors and entered the saloon.

'He's a stranger,' someone observed, as if that accounted for Hart's actions.

'And he ain't got long to live,' the barkeep said.

Hart looked around. Most of the men were young, hard-faced and armed. Two men seated at a small table to the left looked older and were not carrying guns. Hart saw apprehension in their expressions, and decided against using them. He transferred his attention to the barkeep.

'What's your name, mister?' he asked.

'Cy Jenner. If you know what's good for you, you'll haul your freight outa town before Crane hears about this. He said he'd shoot anyone who turned O'Hara loose.'

'O'Hara looks to be in a bad way,' Hart said. 'Take someone with you and fetch him in here to thaw out. Pour some whiskey into him, and then feed him hot food.'

'Not me.' Jenner shook his head emphatically. 'I've seen Crane shoot a man for disobeying him.'

Hart spoke softly. 'I told you what to do and, if it ain't done in two minutes, I'll shoot you. So get to it.'

'Just a cotton-picking minute.' A big man standing with three others at the far end of the bar stepped forward, shrugging his wide shoulders. 'I'm Jake Kenyon, and I run this town when Crane ain't around, see? I say O'Hara stays tied to the rail, and seeing that you cut him loose then you can go tie him up again. And if you don't do like I say, I'll shoot you. We don't like strangers coming into our town and sticking their long noses into our affairs.'

Hart shrugged his bedroll on to the bar and placed his Winchester beside it, aware that he had to make an example of someone in order to cow the others. He faced Kenyon, stripping the glove from his right hand and flexing his fingers.

'You called it,' he said harshly. 'Turn it loose.'

Kenyon's heavy face showed fleeting surprise at the cold-blooded challenge, and then he compressed his lips and reached for his gun in a fast draw. Hart moved in unison, and his pistol seemed to leap into his big right hand. He cocked the weapon before it levelled, and triggered a shot that blasted the silence from the long room. Kenyon staggered back a couple of steps as the bullet punched into the centre of his chest. His half-drawn pistol fell from his hand as he twisted and fell on his face on the hard boards. Gunsmoke drifted across the bar as Hart returned his pistol to its holster.

'Anyone else got orders from Crane and want to die trying to obey them?' he demanded. He paused but no one responded to his challenge. 'OK, Jenner,' he rapped. 'Now you know what the deal is you

16

better do like I told you. Get O'Hara in here.'

The barkeep scurried out from behind the bar, motioned to one of the nearby men to accompany him, and they both hurried to the batwings. Moments later they returned, half-dragging O'Hara with them. The unfortunate Circle M rider was placed on a chair near the stove, and Jenner hurried to the bar for a generous tot of whiskey. Hart remained motionless until O'Hara began to thaw out.

'Give him hot food and then let him be until he's ready to leave,' Hart said.

'You're storing up a load of grief for yourself, stranger, although you don't know it,' Jenner said. 'Crane will tear this town apart to get at you when he hears about this. You ain't got a prayer, mister. The only way you can save yourself is to hightail it outa here.'

'Crane won't have to look far to find me.' Hart smiled. 'I'll be right here. Give me a whiskey, and then get me a big steak with all the trimmings. I'll finish off with a pie, apple, if you've got it, with molasses, and then a pot of coffee. And make it quick. I ain't eaten since dawn, and that is a long, long time in this weather.'

Jenner hurried to obey. He set a bottle of whiskey and a glass in front of Hart, and then almost ran from behind the bar to disappear through a doorway in the back wall. Hart heard him yelling instructions for food to be prepared. Jenner returned moments later, mopping his forehead.

Hart drank two fingers of whiskey. 'Where can I get a good room for the night?' he asked.

'We got rooms,' Jenner replied. 'But I don't know as Crane would let you stay here, under the circumstances.'

'What gives you the idea I'd wanta stay here?' Hart shook his head. 'Is there an undertaker in town? Someone oughta remove that body. I don't want to sit looking at it while I'm eating. Where is Crane? You said he's away. It ain't good weather for making a trip.'

'Business trips are OK in any weather,' Jenner said unhappily. 'Crane reckons to be back tomorrow.'

'So he left after tying O'Hara to the hitch rack, huh? Was O'Hara supposed to remain there until Crane returned?'

'I wouldn't have untied him.' Jenner turned to the nearby men and gave instructions for Kenyon's body to be taken out. Three of them picked up the corpse and departed silently. There was a large bloodstain on the floorboards where the body had fallen and Jenner fetched a bucket of sawdust to obliterate it. The tension that had accrued after the shooting seemed to fade with Kenyon's removal.

'Is there a law man in town?' Hart asked.

'Crane is acting sheriff,' Jenner replied.

'Was he elected?'

'Yeah, by himself. Nobody else wanted the job.'

Hart nodded. He poured another whiskey, looked around the big room, and then picked up the bottle and his glass and moved across to a small table near the door to the kitchen, leaving his bedroll and rifle on the end of the bar. He sat down and watched the room. The men present were on edge, if their expressions were anything to go by. They had witnessed his fast draw, and Kenyon, who had to be very good because of his position in Crane's hierarchy, had not stood a chance from an even break.

Eventually, a woman emerged from the kitchen carrying a big platter containing a two-pound steak, fried eggs and potatoes, and biscuits hot from the stove. Hart murmured his thanks as he was served, and fell to eating when the woman departed, aware that all eyes in the room were upon him. He paused once to draw his pistol and put it on the table close to his right hand. The men who had carried out Kenyon's body did not return, and Hart was mindful of the fact that they might now be outside planning to shoot him when he decided to leave.

The woman returned later with an apple pie and a pitcher of milk. Hart pushed his empty plate aside and set about the pie. He leaned back in his seat with a grunt of appreciation when he was through eating, and thanked the woman again when she came for the dishes.

'You can pay Jenner,' she said, smiling at his thanks.

'That was the best meal I ever ate,' Hart told her as she departed. 'I'll surely have to come again tomorrow.'

'Crane will be back then,' Jenner called, 'and I don't reckon you'll be in a fit state to eat after he gets through with you.'

Hart smiled and went to the bar. He paid for two

meals and the whiskey, and then turned to O'Hara, who was still huddled close to the stove.

'How you feeling, feller?' he demanded.

'Nearly back to normal. Thanks, mister. You saved my life. I wouldn't have lasted much longer out there. I wish you'd leave before Crane comes back.'

'I'm gonna stick around and wait for him to show up,' Hart said. 'But you better head back to your outfit before something else happens.'

'There are some things a man just can't swallow, and there'll be gunsmoke for sure when Crane shows up. I'd like to be here and take a hand in that.'

'I don't want you around.' Hart shook his head. 'I always do my business alone. You better leave while you can.'

'Watch out for the three men who took Kenyon out. Deke Harlan is one of Crane's top hands, and he'll be waiting outside for sure when you leave.'

'Thanks. I already got that worked out.'

Hart picked up his bedroll and rifle and walked to the batwings, pausing when a harsh voice yelled from the darkness outside.

'Come ahead, stranger. We're waiting on you. And come out shooting.'

Hart shifted his rifle to his left hand, drew his pistol, and went out fast. He lunged to his left when he reached the sidewalk, and dropped flat as shooting erupted. Flashes split the night and gun echoes hammered across the uneasy town. Hart was satisfied. He had made a good start on his new chore.

TWO

Hart hit the sidewalk heavily and rolled to his left, thrusting his gun hand forward as slugs came hammering out of the shadows to slam into the front wall of the saloon around him. He fired instinctively at flaring orange flashes, and gun thunder rolled and racketed through the darkness. There were two guns shooting at him from the right and one from over on the left. His hat was jerked by the impact of a slug boring through it, and his reply was to trigger his pistol relentlessly.

Shattering glass sounded, and then a pistol opened fire on the attackers from a front window of the saloon. Hart drove two slugs into a gun flash to his right and the weapon stopped shooting. At that moment the second gun on the right also stopped firing. Hart transferred his attention to the left, and was involved in an exchange of shots until one of his slugs struck home and the ambusher dropped out of it.

Hart listened to the fading echoes of the shooting. He shook his head ruefully. It hadn't taken him long to find trouble. But he had to make a start some-where, and a man who would tie another out in this weather and leave him to die of exposure just had to be involved in the trouble hereabouts. He was satis-fied that he was on the right track, and would talk to Bart Crane when the saloon man returned.

'I think we got them all,' O'Hara called from the window he had broken to join in the fight.

Hart got to his feet and retrieved his gear. O'Hara emerged through the batwings. He was grinning. He had a gunbelt buckled around his waist, and thrust the pistol he was holding into the holster.

'I got my gun back from Jenner,' he said. 'Maybe we oughter stick together until morning. I'll be riding out then. But things being what they are, I just got to stick around until Crane gets back.'

'Seems like a good idea.' Hart glanced around the street. Men were peering from various buildings; skulking in the shadows. 'Tell Jenner to bring a lamp out here so I can check out the shooting.'

He stood with his back to the front wall of the saloon, peering around alertly, and a few moments later Jenner emerged cautiously from the saloon with a lantern in his hand. Hart leaned his rifle against the front wall of the saloon and put his bedroll beside it.

'Walk slowly across the street, Jenner,' Hart said. 'I'll follow you. I think we nailed three guns that opened up on me, and I need to check them out.'

'I ain't got anything to do with this,' Jenner protested.

'Complain to Crane when you see him,' Hart retorted. 'Get moving.'

Jenner shielded the lantern with an up-flung arm and started across the street. Hart followed him, pistol ready for action. He guided Jenner with softly called instructions, and they came upon two bodies lying in an alley mouth opposite. Both men were dead, and Hart recognized them as being two of the three men who had carried Kenyon's body out of the saloon.

'What are their names?' Hart asked.

'This one is Downey, and that one is Parr.'

'Walk to the left now,' Hart directed. 'There was another gun firing from over there.'

The wind tugged at them as they moved. A door was rattling frenziedly under the power of the ceaseless gusts that were racking the town. Hart watched his surroundings. The dim light from the lamp was barely adequate, and cast dense shadows around, but they found a spot where blood stained the ground, although there was no sign of a body.

'He got away with it, but he won't get far,' Hart mused. 'He's lost a lot of blood. Is there a doctor in town?'

'Doc Chilvers. He's got an office next to the bank.' Jenner spoke sullenly. 'Can I go now?'

'Yeah. Make yourself scarce. I'll be around tomorrow to check on that third man. What is his name?'

'Deke Harlan was the third man who helped take Kenyon's body out of the saloon, but I don't know if he was mixed up in shooting at you.'

'He should be easy to trace. I'll get to him.'

Hart stood and watched Jenner go back into the saloon. O'Hara came across the street, carrying Hart's bedroll and rifle. Hart named the two men who had been killed, and O'Hara nodded.

'I'm not surprised. Crane has been getting away with murder around here. The way they handled me proves they are capable of anything. But you've pulled Crane up on a short rein, and he ain't gonna like that.'

'By the time he gets back to town he might be running short of men,' Hart observed. 'Where can we hit the sack tonight?'

'The hay loft in the livery barn is open to us, and it won't cost a cent.' O'Hara nodded. 'And we'll be close to our horses if we need to quit town fast.'

'I need to get to A Bar M tomorrow. You can show me the way, huh?'

'It'll be a pleasure. My boss and the boss of A Bar M are brothers; Art and Ben Murdock. Are you looking for a riding job?'

Hart shook his head. 'No. I got other fish to fry,' he said.

They went along to the stable. The ostler, Nat Askew, was standing in the shadows inside the big front entrance. He was holding a double-barrelled shotgun, the butt tucked in his right armpit and the fearsome twin muzzles pointing at the ground. He lowered the weapon when he recognized Hart.

'What was that shooting about?' he demanded.

O'Hara told him and Askew chuckled when he

learned that they planned to bed down in the barn.

'Help yourselves,' he said. 'Anyone who gives trouble to Bart Crane is a friend of mine. So Kenyon is dead, huh? And Downey and Parr. You must be pretty slick on the draw to beat Kenyon from an even break, stranger. I always fancied that one day someone would come along and make him look real slow. The other two were just gun-bullies. They never amounted to much.'

Hart made no comment and, while O'Hara climbed the loft ladder to sleep in the hay stored there, he entered the stall where his horse was spending the night and rolled himself in his blankets in a corner. He slept comfortably despite the banging of a loose board in the roof, and awakened next morning to the sound of rain driving across the town.

O'Hara was in the stable office chatting with Askew when Hart showed himself. Askew had a coffee pot on the stove, and poured Hart a cup of the strong liquid.

'Have you got any idea where Bart Crane has gone?' Hart asked.

'He rode out around eleven. Kenyon came for Crane's grey stallion, and I saw Crane leaving a little later.' Askew shook his head. 'I got no idea where he was heading. He rode south, which doesn't tell us much because he probably cleared town and then changed direction.'

'Does he often leave town?' Hart asked.

'I've seen him on the range many times,' O'Hara said.

Askew shook his head. 'I've never watched his comings and goings, but he rides out at all times, although I've never known him to stay away overnight before. He doesn't trust his hired men, and maybe he's right, at that. I wouldn't trust any of them further than I could throw them.'

'Does he own property outside of town?' Hart persisted.

'He's got a couple of small ranches out west run by tenants; wide-loopers, by the look of them, and, of course, he's interested in Widow Baines, who owns the JB ranch. He often rides out there to see her.'

'He wants to buy that place,' O'Hara said. 'That's his only interest in Mrs Baines. I heard he's pestering the life out of her and, if she doesn't sell before long, bad things will start to happen around her. Crane ran Charlie Halloran out like that, and Charlie had to sell to him because Crane scared off any other would-be buyers. Henry Davis, the banker, told my boss that Crane warned him against advancing money to anyone who wanted to buy out Charlie. And guess what happened to Charlie? He was drygulched after he sold, and the money he got for his ranch was stolen.'

'And McGee never got a pointer to that business.' Askew shook his head. 'The sheriff was shot dead the minute he started asking questions around town.'

'So that was why the sheriff was killed, huh?' Hart was beginning to get a picture in his mind, and did not like its implications.

'That's it. No one stands up against Crane and gets

26

away with it.' O'Hara looked into Hart's eyes. 'So you know what you can expect when Crane learns about Kenyon. He won't let you live in case others get ideas about standing up to him. That's how Crane does his business.'

'I reckon it's time to eat,' Hart said softly. 'Then I need to ride out. I'll come back to see Crane when I can get around to him.'

'And I'll be waiting to witness that meeting,' Askew said eagerly.

'There's a hash house along the street,' O'Hara suggested. 'They'll be serving breakfast right now.'

'Can you tell me anything about the bank robbery that happened about six months ago?' Hart asked, as they walked along the sidewalk.

'I heard talk about it, but there was nothing definite beyond the fact that four strangers rode in. One of them stayed outside the bank holding their horses while the other three went inside and lifted the dough. It was a slick job. They worked like it wasn't the first time they'd hit a bank.'

Hart's thoughts ran deep while he ate breakfast. Captain Buckbee hadn't underestimated the degree of lawlessness that was rife in this county. It would be a case of shooting down the opposition until none was left. Some cases were like that. He did not need to hunt for the guilty men because they were there for the taking. His nerves tightened at the thought of impending action.

'You didn't tell me why Crane had you tied to the hitch rack,' Hart said, as he drank his coffee.

'Crane ain't got anything personal against me,' O'Hara grimaced. 'He grabbed me because I ride for Circle M. He's stayed away from trouble with the Murdock brothers because they're too big to buck. But lately he's been pawing the ground in their direction, and it looks like he's about ready to take them on.'

Hart got to his feet. 'We better split the breeze. The wind seems to have an extra bite to it this morning. I'd like to get done around here before the snow flies. I want to be back in San Antonio by Christmas.'

'The snow won't be long in coming,' O'Hara agreed. 'I've been riding this range for a lot of years, and I can smell snow in the wind. Another week or so at most and you'll need wings on your horse to get around.'

They went out to the street, and O'Hara uttered an imprecation when he saw eight riders coming into town from the north.

'Heck, that's my boss along there. What's he brought the hard bunch in for?'

'The hard bunch?' Hart queried.

'They're the gunnies the boss hired because of trouble brewing,' O'Hara said. 'I should have gone back to the ranch yesterday. I reckon they're here because I didn't show up at Circle M.'

They walked towards the group, who were halting in front of the livery barn. Hart could see Askew standing in the doorway, talking and nodding emphatically. The foremost rider was a big man with a heavy raw-boned frame who was dressed in good

28

range clothes. He was astride a buckskin, Hart noted, as they drew nearer to the barn.

'That's the boss, Ben Murdock, talking to Askew,' O'Hara said. 'I got a good idea what he's gonna say and do when he learns what happened to me yesterday.'

One of the riders spotted O'Hara and spoke to Murdock, who twisted in his saddle, then reined his horse around and came swiftly to where Hart and O'Hara had paused, followed closely by his men.

'Is it true what Askew told me, Pete?' Ben Murdock had sandy hair that showed at his temples under the brim of his grey Stetson. His eyes were blue, glinting with anger, and there was a rasping note in his harsh voice. 'Did Crane have you roped to his hitch rack yesterday?'

'Yeah, Boss, for most of the day, until this man turned me loose.'

Hart was being regarded with a cold, impersonal gaze by the riders flanking Murdoch. He could tell at a glance that they were hired guns. He studied Ben Murdoch. The Circle M rancher was in his early fifties and looked as tough as whang leather, his weathered face mottled by the extremes of heat and cold to which it had been subjected through the seasons over many years. His lips were pinched as he fought to control his anger.

'Hank, you and Bender get along to the saloon and grab any of Crane's men you find there. If Kenyon gives you any trouble then you got my permission to shoot him.'

'Hold it!' O'Hara was shaking his head. 'You're too late, Boss. Kenyon's dead, and so are Downey and Parr. Deke Harlan was bad hit and ain't been seen since. I reckon he's crawled into some hole in town to die.'

'What in hell has been going on around here?' Murdock demanded.

Hart stood silent while O'Hara explained, and the impersonal eyes of the hired guns filled with interest as the narration unfolded. By the time O'Hara had described the fight outside the saloon, Murdock was smiling, his pale eyes gleaming with appreciation.

'Hank, go talk to Doc Chilvers. See if Harlan paid him a visit. Bring Harlan to me, if you find him.'

Two of the riders moved away along the street. Ben Murdock stepped down from his saddle. He was tall, and looked formidable with a pistol holstered on his right hip.

'It's about time we did something about Crane and his set-up,' he mused. 'What's your name, feller?' His cold grey eyes bored into Hart.

'Mike Hart.'

'You looking for a job? I could certainly do with a man like you.'

'I'm riding out to A Bar M this morning,' Hart said.

'Are you going to work for my brother?'

'I'm not going to work for anyone. I've been sent here to do a job.'

'Are you a lawman? Crane had the last sheriff murdered. I can't prove that, but I sure as hell know

30

he was responsible.'

'I ride with the Texas Rangers,' Hart said. 'Captain Buckbee, in San Antonio, sent me up here to sort out the trouble.'

'One man?' Murdock shook his head. 'Heck, it'll take a whole company of Rangers to handle our problems. Apart from the trouble Crane causes around here, we got rustlers on the range, and there's a gang of bank robbers mixed up in it somewhere. I heard that the bunch who hit the bank here six months ago held up a stage over Rio Verde way last week, killing the driver and two passengers. They got away with two thousand dollars. Say, my brother is friendly with Ed Buckbee. Is that why you're here? Did Art send for help?'

'I wouldn't know about that.' Hart spoke softly. 'I'm here because I was ordered to come, and I would like to point out that I can't stand by and watch anyone breaking the law, or taking the law into their own hands. I suggest you hold off for a little longer, whatever problems you've had in the past, and I'll get on with my job and sort it out.'

'Just one man?' Ben Murdock repeated, shaking his head. 'Say, it would be worth it to hold fire and see just what kind of a mess you make of this situation.'

'He ain't done too badly so far, Boss,' O'Hara reminded.

'Beginner's luck.' Murdock glanced around the street. 'OK, Hart, I'll call off my dogs and give you a chance to prove yourself. I'll leave Pete to ride with you over the next couple of days. He'll know where

31

to bring you when you decide that you can do with some help. My brother out at A Bar M doesn't see eye to eye with me on the way to fight the trouble we've got. I believe in fighting fire with fire. I'm loaded for bear now, and the next bit of trouble we get on this range will find me coming in to flush out Crane and his bunch.'

'You'll be the first man I'll run to if I need help,' Hart said.

Murdock lifted his pistol from its holster and fired a shot into the air. His two riders along the street, now reining up in front of the doctor's house, swung around, and Murdock signalled for them to return.

'See you back at the ranch in a couple of days, Pete,' Murdock said. 'Give Hart what help you can before you leave him.'

'Sure, Boss.' O'Hara grinned happily. 'I was hoping you'd say that.'

'Be seeing you, Hart.' Murdock swung into his saddle and turned his horse to ride out of town, followed by his tough outfit.

'He's a good man,' O'Hara said. 'He won't take any guff from Crane. I got the feeling now that Crane's days are numbering mighty low.'

'I don't need you to ride herd on me, Pete,' Hart said. 'I can even find my way to A Bar M without a guide. But you can ride with me for a spell, and I'll learn what I can about the events that have occurred around here over the past six months.'

'Are you gonna visit Crane's saloon before we ride out of town?'

'No. It wouldn't serve any useful purpose while Crane is away. I'll drop in on Crane when I know he's at home. Let's ride out to A Bar M.'

They entered the stable and prepared their horses for travel. Hart, keen to get to grips with his assignment, was aware that a number of leads had to be followed up, but at the moment he had only a hazy idea what to tackle first, although he knew by experience that his priorities would sort themselves out as he continued. But he needed to see Art Murdock, and had decided to visit A Bar M without delay.

They rode out at a canter, the wind tugging at them as they headed along a well-defined trail that led generally in a north-west direction. Hart could sense the onset of winter. The wind seemed to have an added bite to its breath this morning, and the sky was tinged lead-grey, heralding snow in the near future.

'You said you've been on this range a long time, Pete,' Hart mused. He had pulled his neckerchief up over his nose and mouth to protect them from the cold air. 'I want to know what's going on under the surface in the county. Who is after what? Crane I know about. But there must be others around who are trying to turn events to their own advantage.'

'That's a hard question to answer.' O'Hara grimaced. 'I'd stake my life on the Murdock brothers. I know for a fact that my boss ain't got any irons in the fire that you'd be interested in, and his brother Art is a great one for minding his own business. Between them, they handle the biggest herd in this part of the world. I reckon it takes them all their time to keep an eye on what they have got.'

'I can understand that.' Hart nodded. 'What else is going on around here?'

'Pat Gedge is a farmer. A bunch of them sodbusters have settled in the Coulee Hills on land that ain't good for cattle. Gedge is a stirrer. He ain't satisfied with poor land, and would like to move in on cattle range, which means taking over Circle M or A Bar M range. It ain't gonna happen, because Ben and Art Murdock have given strict orders to their crews – anyone finding farmers moving on to Murdock grass must chase 'em off with gunsmoke.'

'You've been given the word to use force?' Hart grimaced as he thought about it. This situation was a whole lot worse than he had figured.

'Sure thing. I was with the riders Ben Murdock led over to Coulee Hills some months ago, and I heard him lay down the law to Gedge, who I don't cotton to. He's a loud-mouth – got one of the biggest farms in the Hills, but if he does any serious farming then I'll eat my hat. He's got a couple of tough men in to do his work because he's too busy riding around getting the other farmers to stand up to the ranchers. Any bad blood between the two factions was raised by Pat Gedge. I don't know why he wants a war, because the farmers couldn't win it nohow.'

Hart grimaced. The more he heard about local events the more he realized that they were being shaped by a few men who were determined to profit from trouble. The pattern was beginning to emerge, and he held down his impatience as they rode at a mile-eating lope towards the distant hills in the north-west.

Around noon, O'Hara reined in on a rise and pointed off to the left. Hart glanced in that direction and saw a small ranch situated by a creek. There was a house, one barn, and a corral.

'That's the JB spread,' O'Hara said. 'Widow Baines runs it. We could stop off there for grub and coffee. What do you say?'

'Sure thing. I'll need to meet Mrs Baines, and there's no time like the present.'

They changed direction and approached the cluster of buildings.

'Say, there's a lot of activity in the yard,' O'Hara observed. 'What's going on? Miz Baines has only three men riding for her, but there are a dozen horses standing in front of the house.'

Hart had spotted the horses, and reached into a saddle-bag for his field-glasses. He handed them to O'Hara, who adjusted them to his eyes and scanned the ranch.

'Talk of the devil,' O'Hara said softly. 'Pat Gedge is on the porch with the widow, and those men with him are dirt farmers. I can see Bill Thompson and Snapper Mason, a couple of close friends of Gedge. What in blazes are they doing out here? They don't generally leave the Hills.'

'Let's ride in there and find out.' Hart returned the glasses to his saddle-bag.

'It sure looks like trouble for the widow,' O'Hara mused.

They went on at a fast run, and Hart's gaze passed over the assembled men as he and O'Hara reached the yard. Three men were standing on the porch with a middle-aged woman, who was looking flustered. The sound of approaching hoofs alerted the farmers, and they turned to watch Hart and O'Hara ride in. Hart noted that the farmers were armed, some with rifles on their saddles or wearing holstered pistols.

'That's Pat Gedge wearing the red jacket,' O'Hara said, as they reined up in front of the house. 'He'll be running things.'

Hart studied the big, powerfully built man standing head and shoulders over the woman. From his attitude, Hart was certain Gedge had been threatening Mrs Baines. Gedge was an ugly man. His eyes were close together, and small, giving him the look of a weasel. His mouth was cruel; lips pressed together in a thin line.

'What do you want, O'Hara?' Gedge demanded angrily. 'What are you poking your long nose in here for?'

'I'm just showing this Texas Ranger around the range,' O'Hara replied. 'He's come to end the trouble honest folk are getting.'

Hart saw the expression of relief which came to the woman's face at the news, and he pulled his right glove off his hand and flexed his fingers.

'What's going on here?' he demanded. 'Are you having problems, ma'am?'

'I've asked these men to leave but they won't

budge,' Mrs Baines said worriedly. 'Gedge has been pestering the life out of me. If you are a Ranger, perhaps you'll help me.'

'With pleasure.' Hart was watching the assembled farmers closely, and spotted one man who seemed to be out of place among the sodbusters. He was wearing twin gunbelts, and looked like a smokeroo ready to draw and shoot. The man began to pull his right-hand gun, and Hart flowed into action.

THREE

The gunman was swinging in his saddle to line up his pistol on Hart when the Ranger drew fast and fired a single shot. The slug narrowly missed a farmer, whose body was half covering Hart's target, before thumping into the gunman's chest. Echoes fled across the yard as the man pitched from his saddle and fell heavily to the ground. Several of the farmers reached instinctively for their weapons, but froze when Hart called a sharp warning.

Pat Gedge and the two men on the porch turned angry faces to Hart, who gigged his mount forward a few steps.

'Quit the porch, Gedge,' Hart said crisply, 'and make it quick.'

Gedge opened his mouth as if to protest, but Hart's levelled gun forestalled argument. Gedge was the first to move. He clumped off the porch and grasped the reins of his horse.

'Pick up your man and put him back in his saddle,' Hart rapped. 'He's still alive, so you better take care of him before he bleeds to death.'

Pete O'Hara had snaked his pistol from its holster and was lending weight to Hart's play. An uneasy silence settled over the ranch as the farmers pulled out, and O'Hara heaved an audible sigh when the last of them disappeared from sight. Hart holstered his pistol and stepped down from his saddle. He was smiling as he confronted the shaken woman on the porch.

'Would you mind telling me what that was all about, ma'am?' Hart asked.

'Pat Gedge came with a warning about trouble coming to me unless I sold out to him. He was real nice to start with, but, when I refused to consider selling, he turned nasty. I don't know what would have happened if you and Pete hadn't showed up when you did.'

'Gedge offered to buy you out?' O'Hara echoed, shaking his head. 'Where would he get that kind of money from? Farmers never have two dollars to rub together.'

'He said the farmers had raised it between them. They want to move in here and start farming; turn this good grazing land under the plough.' Mrs Baines shook her head emphatically. 'My husband would turn in his grave if I even considered selling under those circumstances. The first thing the sodbusters would do is put up fences. I wouldn't even sell to Bart Crane, and he wanted to run cattle here.'

'Have you seen Crane around in the last twenty-four hours?' Hart asked.

'No. He was out here last week, trying to buy me

out. He said he's in no hurry, and gave me time to think it over. I don't want to sell, but I'm getting tired of the trouble that seems to be raising its head around here. We've had some steers run off, and there was a prowler several nights ago, making noises out there in the dark. But I don't scare easy. I sleep with my husband's pistol to hand, and I'd use it if I had to.'

'I think I can promise you some easement of your trouble in the near future.' Hart's blue eyes held a bleak expression as he glanced around. 'Where are your riders? Pete tells me you've got three men on your payroll.'

'They rode out at dawn to bring our cattle in closer to the ranch. I don't think many more days will pass before we see the first snow of the winter. I can feel it in my bones.' Mrs Baines shrugged. Strain was showing in her wrinkled face. 'Would you care to come in and sit and eat? I was making coffee when Gedge and those sodbusters showed up.'

'Thank you, ma'am,' Hart replied. 'I was of a mind to take advantage of your hospitality when I rode up, but in view of what happened here I guess I'd better be on my way. Perhaps Pete can stay on for a spell.'

'I could stay until your riders get back, just in case Gedge and his friends decide to return,' O'Hara said, frowning. 'Perhaps you shouldn't stay out here alone, Miz Baines. It might be safer for you in town until the Ranger gets to grips with the problems he's facing.'

'No one is gonna run me out. My husband stood

firm, and I'll not be found wanting.'

Hart considered for a moment. He wanted to talk to Gedge, but not while the man was heading a dozen farmers, and was aware that he could always drop on to Gedge. He was pondering what course of action to take. Until now he had gained the impression that the trouble hereabouts was being instigated by Bart Crane. But Gedge formed another facet that had to be considered, and this lonely woman needed protection.

'Is there anyone in town you could stay with for a few days?' Hart asked.

Mrs Baines shook her head, and Hart forestalled her inevitable reply.

'The trouble is, I'm not inclined to leave you out here alone while I pursue Gedge and get to the bottom of his actions, and I have several other things to do that are high on my list of actions.'

'I understand, but you don't have to worry about me,' Mrs Baines assured him. 'I can defend this place as well as any man.'

'I'll stay here until your three riders return,' O'Hara said. He glanced at Hart. 'If you want to go to A Bar M then pick up the trail about two hundred yards over there beyond the creek, and follow it to the north-west. Art Murdock's place is three hours' ride from here.'

'Thanks. I'll be seeing you again, Mrs Baines. When your riders do return, you'd better make sure that one of them is always on the spread.'

'I will.' The woman nodded emphatically.

'Everything has changed with Gedge's visit this morning. He was actually threatening me.'

'He won't bother you again,' Hart promised. 'I'll have a word with him, and that should be sufficient to hold him back.'

O'Hara grinned as Hart turned away. Hart crossed to where Gedge's horse had stood and dropped to one knee to examine the hoof prints there. An expert tracker, he studied the prints until he was certain he could recognize them again, and then mounted and prepared to ride out. He lifted a hand in a farewell salute and followed Gedge's tracks until he was out of sight of the ranch house.

The tracks of the group of farmers were heading towards Ashville and, for a moment, Hart hesitated, trying to decide which of his actions should have priority. Then he noticed that two of the farmers had left the group and were riding north. Checking their hoof prints, Hart recognized one set as belonging to Gedge's mount, and set a fast pace in pursuit in the hope of turning the situation to his advantage. In a matter of minutes he spotted two riders ahead, and recognized one of them as Pat Gedge.

The leader of the farming community reined in and swung his horse about when he heard the rapid beat of Hart's horse, and both farmers halted to wait stolidly for Hart's arrival. Hart stopped before them, holding his reins in his left hand. His right hand, minus his glove, was lying on his right thigh close to the butt of his gun.

'What do you want?' Gedge demanded truculently.

'A few straight answers from you,' Hart countered.

'I got nothing to say to you.' Gedge jerked on his reins to turn his horse away, and then halted the movement for Hart's pistol had appeared in his hand and was pointing unerringly at Gedge's chest.

Gedge's companion immediately lifted his hands shoulder high.

'If you're carrying any weapons then now is the time to get rid of them,' Hart said quietly. 'That goes for you, too,' Hart's keen gaze flickered to Gedge's tough-looking companion. 'Disarm yourselves.'

Gedge looked as if he wanted to disobey but Hart's levelled pistol was master of the situation. Both farmers produced pistols and dropped them, then raised their hands.

'Put your hands down,' Hart rapped. 'Now tell me your reason for being at the Baines ranch this morning.'

'I was wanting to buy the place, if it is any of your business.'

'I'm making it my business. I find it hard to believe that you're planning to buy the ranch. Farmers ain't ever welcome on cattle range, and you're trying to buy a spread set between two of the biggest ranches in the county. So what gives? Are you planning on cattle ranching or are you thinking of turning to farming?'

'We aim to give farming a foothold here. The cattle ranchers have it too much their own way.' Gedge spoke in a surly manner, aware that he could not ride on until Hart was satisfied.

'You know better than that.' Hart's gaze bored into Gedge narrowed eyes. 'No farmer in his right mind would try to do what you're planning, and we both know it. So what's behind your actions? You know you would set the range ablaze if you went ahead, so is that what you're after? You want trouble between the cattlemen and the farmers?'

'That's the last thing I want.' Gedge shook his head angrily. 'We want to buy the ranch and turn it to farming. What's wrong with that? What are you getting so het up about?'

'You'd be declaring war on cattlemen, and from where I'm standing that looks like a fool venture. You couldn't win nohow. The cowmen would stomp you into the dust. So what's the real reason behind you? I don't think you'd be trying anything like that for yourself. You must be working for someone else.'

'I don't know what you mean.'

'I think you do.' Hart's tone was harsh. 'You've got to be acting for someone else. From what I know of farmers, they couldn't raise the price of a few extra acres, so where do you come from, trying to buy a ranch?'

'That's our business, Ranger, and we don't need any long-nose lawman coming in here questioning us.'

'Get out of here.' Hart spoke roughly, aware that he was wasting time. 'Ride out now, and don't go near the Baines ranch again or I'll put you behind bars.'

Gedge looked like he wanted to object, but the steady muzzle of Hart's pistol gaping at him filled

him with caution and he whirled his horse and rode
on. His companion gazed at Hart for a moment
longer before following. Hart sat watching them
until they were out of sight, and then moved away
west to pick up the trail to A Bar M. He paused
behind the nearest ridge and watched the spot where
he had confronted Gedge, expecting the farmers to
return for their pistols, but they kept going.

Hart was of a mind to follow Gedge, but the situation was such that he decided to go on to A Bar M.
He cut across the narrow trail leading to Art
Murdock's ranch and pushed along fast. It was about
the middle of the afternoon when he reached the
rim of a long, curving valley that came down from
the Coulee Hills, and saw a cluster of ranch buildings
beside a creek that was fed by a meandering stream
running the length of the valley. A big herd of cattle
was moving slowly down the valley from Hart's left,
with several riders around them, keeping them
moving. It looked like the herd was being brought on
to home range because of the threat of snow.

Hart rode along the rim to the right until he
found a trail descending to the valley floor, which he
followed into the ranch. A rider came towards him
from behind a barn as he passed through the big
gateway into the yard, and he was met before he
could reach the ranch house. The rider was wearing
a holstered pistol and carried a rifle in his right
hand. He looked mean and resolute.

'You got business here, mister?' the guard
demanded.

'Sure. I need to talk to Art Murdock,' Hart replied.

'You can't see him. He was shot this morning. He was standing on the porch when a bullet took him through the chest. It was fired from beyond the creek. The doctor has just arrived, and it looks like the boss might not live. What's your business?'

Hart frowned at the news. 'Did the ambusher get away?' he asked.

'Two of the men are following his tracks. He lit out fast after the shooting.'

'I'm Mike Hart, Texas Ranger. Art Murdock was expecting me to show up. He was in touch with Captain Buckbee in San Antonio. Who can I talk to now?'

'There's only the ranch foreman, Hemp Benteen, but we've sent word to Ben Murdock at Circle M, who's brother to the boss, and he'll be riding in shortly. I reckon he'll take over here until Art is on his feet again. Ride over to the house. You'll find Benteen there, running things.'

Hart went on to the house, and as he reached the porch a big man emerged from the house to confront him.

'What do you want?' he demanded.

'You're Benteen?'

'I sure wish I wasn't at this moment.' Benteen was heavily built on a large frame, with wide shoulders and powerful arms. Despite the cold wind he was in shirt sleeves, which were rolled high on his arms to reveal well developed biceps. A cartridge belt encircled his thick waist, and a .45 Remington pistol was holstered on his right hip. He was a man in his early forties, with a fleshy face adorned with bushy black eyebrows and a thick black moustache. His expression was fierce, his tone impatient and harsh.

'I'm Mike Hart, Texas Ranger.' Hart noticed the momentary narrowing of Benteen's eyes, and then the foreman nodded.

'You're expected,' he grated. 'The boss was getting impatient because you hadn't showed up. It's a pity you weren't here earlier.'

'I got here soon as I could. I heard about Art getting shot. What does the doctor say about him?'

'Doc Chilvers is still with him. He took a slug out of Art's chest, and thinks the boss will pull through. You better come into the house and talk to Charlie, Art's daughter. She says she's gonna run things around here until the boss is up and about again.'

Hart dismounted and stepped on to the porch. Benteen turned to lead the way into the house but a tall, slender girl of about twenty-five years appeared in the big doorway and gazed curiously at Hart. She was dressed in range clothes – red shirt, blue denim pants and brown riding boots. Her long blonde hair was dishevelled, as if she had been out in the wind without a hat.

'Here's the Ranger your dad has been waiting for,' Benteen said. 'I've told him what's happened.'

'I'm Mike Hart. Sorry to hear about your father, Miss Murdock.'

The sound of rapidly approaching hoofs cut across the introductions. Hart turned swiftly to see three

47

riders coming across the yard towards the house, and one of them was face-down across his saddle. Benteen uttered a smothered curse and went hurriedly off the porch to stop the riders coming in closer. Charlene Murdock stiffened, a hand going to her mouth in shock.

'That's Joe Roper and Will Rankin,' she said quickly. 'They rode out on the trail of the man who shot Dad.'

'It looks like they got him,' Hart observed, and went quickly behind Benteen to hear the report from the approaching riders.

'What happened, Joe?' Benteen demanded, as the riders reined in. He walked to the body slung across the third horse. 'Anyone we know?'

'I've seen him around town once or twice,' Roper said. 'He's a drifter, I reckon. We had to kill him. He turned nasty when we caught up with him.'

Benteen grasped the dead man's hair and lifted the head to look at the pallid face. 'Yeah,' he observed. I've seen him around. You sure he's the one who shot the boss?'

'Yep. Tracked him to the spot where we killed him. How's the boss?'

'The doc reckons he's tough enough to survive this. Put the body in the barn for now.' Benteen glanced at Hart. 'This is the Ranger we been expecting. He'll likely wanta talk to you.'

'Have you searched him?' Hart asked, as he accompanied Roper across the yard to the barn while Rankin went across to the cook shack.

'No. Didn't think that was necessary. We got him, and that's all we care about.'

'It would have been better if you'd taken him alive,' Hart said.

'Yeah, but lead started flying, and our main aim was to stop him getting away.' Joe Roper was old for a cowpuncher, looking to be in his fifties, with a grizzled face and narrowed brown eyes. He grinned when he met Hart's level gaze, and tension drained out of him. 'There are a lot like him showing up around the range,' he added. 'You don't need to know their names. They all come from the same mould. Trouble attracts them, and there sure is plenty of that on the way. We are covering all directions, and still can't see where it is coming from. Even Ashville ain't the same no more, what with Crane taking over everything.'

They lifted the body from the saddle and carried it into the barn. Hart crouched over the dead man and searched his pockets carefully, but found little of note – only a roll of dollar bills and some loose gold coins, but nothing to aid the identification of the body.

'What's he doing with that amount of money on him?' Roper asked. 'A drifter like him wouldn't have the price of a meal. His kind live by riding the chuck-line.'

'It looks like someone paid him to shoot Art Murdock,' Hart said.

'Don't forget his saddle-bags,' Roper added.

Hart stuffed the dead man's belongings into his

pocket and went outside to check the saddle-bags, finding nothing to point to the man's identity.

'Looks like he was prepared for the worst,' Roper commented. 'You'll have to ask around town about him.'

'I'm heading back there shortly,' Hart said. 'I'll take him in.'

Hart went back to the house. Charlene Murdock was standing on the porch, gazing moodily across the yard. She stirred when he reached her, and smiled instinctively, although the worry in her eyes did not lessen. She sighed heavily and shook her head as she studied Hart's grim face.

'It looks like the ambusher was paid to come in and shoot your father,' Hart told her. 'Has he got any enemies you can name?'

'If I gave you the names of everyone in the county I might still miss out one or two who'd like to put a slug in Dad,' she replied bitterly. 'Those farmers up in the hills for a start. They're itching to move down on the range, and they've tried it a couple of times. Our men have had to chase them off. There's a man named Gedge who's agitating the farmers. He's supposed to be a farmer himself, but two men run his farm and he never turns his hand to any work. He's too busy riding around getting others to do his dirty work.'

'I've met Gedge, and what you tell me about him sure fits in with the impression I got.' Hart narrated the incident at the Baines ranch, and saw alarm show in Charlene's eyes.

'I've been worried about Martha for a long time,' she said, and turned and called for Benteen, who emerged from the house. She repeated what Hart had told her, and Benteen shook his head. 'Send three men over to JB to guard the spread,' she continued. 'They'd better stay there until this trouble is over. I said we should have done something before. Now, get men over there before anything worse happens.'

'I'll get on to it right away.' Benteen went off across the yard.

'I'm taking over the reins here while my father is recovering,' Charlene said, and there was resolution in the set of her mouth.

'Have you seen anything of Bart Crane in the last twenty-four hours?' Hart queried.

She laughed harshly. 'This is the last place he'd show up. Our men would tear him to pieces. We have a tough job controlling them as it is. Dad has said he'll fire anyone who causes any trouble with Crane. It's got so bad for them in Ashville that the majority of them ride an extra thirty miles in the other direction to Elm Ridge. I think all our troubles started when Crane moved into Ashville.'

Hart told her about finding Pete O'Hara tied to the hitch rack in town, and how Ben Murdock, on learning of the incident, had been prepared to take on Crane but had agreed to give the law a chance to save the situation. The girl's face paled at the news and she shook her head.

'This situation is like a powder keg with a lighted

fuse,' Hart observed.

'I've sent a man to tell Uncle Ben about Dad,' Charlene replied. 'He's always wanted to lock horns with Crane but Dad held him back. Now, I guess, he'll do something about Crane. There'll be no holding him with Pa like to die.'

Hart looked around the ranch. Benteen was over by the bunkhouse, giving orders to three of the crew. Then he spotted four riders coming towards the ranch from up the valley, skirting the herd being driven towards the ranch headquarters.

'Riders coming,' he said.

Charlene frowned as she looked at the newcomers. 'It must be Uncle Ben,' she said at length. 'I'd know his horse anywhere. I'll have a tough fight on my hands to stop him going to war. Would you back me if he does show fight?'

'All the way,' Hart replied. 'I don't want a war any more than you do. If I get the chance, I'll soon get to the root of this trouble and take care of it.'

'But you're just one man! Crane could put twenty men against you. They'd ride over you like a stampeding herd.'

'I expect they would, if I gave them the chance.' Hart smiled. 'But I don't work for a stand-up fight. I'll take them on piece-meal and work my way through them.'

They watched the riders drawing closer, and then Charlene uttered a cry.

'That's Uncle Ben's horse,' she said, 'but it's not him in the saddle.'

The next instant the riders were spurring into the yard and guns began to hammer as they deployed and opened up at the A Bar M crew.

FOUR

The riders split up into two pairs as they entered the yard. Two rode to the right and the others swung to the left, separating to circle the house. They fired rapidly, and Hart paused only to pull Charlene flat to the boards of the porch as he drew his pistol. Then his big Colt hammered, and the first shot downed the leading rider of the pair going to the left. The man threw up his arms and twisted sharply as he fell out of the saddle to thump into the dust and roll lifelessly. Bullets began to smack into the front wall of the house, splintering and gouging the woodwork.

Hart fired two shots at the remaining rider on the left, aware that the two on the right were moving towards the spot where Benteen and a couple of cowpunchers were standing. His shots thudded into the body of the rider, who fell over backwards, his right foot slipping out of the stirrup. His left foot was caught and held, and his head and shoulders bounced through the dust of the yard as his horse dragged him away from the house.

Rolling on to his left side, Hart raised his gun to

54

take on the riders going to the right, and lowered the weapon again when he saw that both men were down. Benteen was on one knee, smoking gun uplifted, and Roper, one of the 'punchers, was already running forward to where the two raiders were lying motionless.

Hart got to his feet, his hard gaze sweeping the surrounding area. There were no other signs of trouble, and he exhaled sharply as he listened to the gun echoes fading slowly into the vast distance. He was aware of Charlene regaining her feet at his side, and threw a glance at her. She was white-faced and shocked, her lips moving soundlessly. Her hand trembled as she reached out and grasped a porch post for support.

'What is happening?' she demanded. 'First Dad, and now this.'

'Get under cover, just in case there are more of them around, and I'll check with Benteen. He might know some of these men.'

Charlene nodded and turned instantly to enter the house. Hart glanced at the two men he had shot, knowing that they were dead. He walked across the yard to where Roper was being joined by Benteen, and both men stood and stared at the motionless figures in the dust.

'Any idea who they are?' Hart called as he reached them.

Benteen looked up at Hart, his heavy face filled with anger. He shook his head in reply, reloading the empty chambers of his pistol from the loops on his cartridge belt. Roper heaved a great sigh as he holstered his pistol. He turned and looked towards the corral near the bunkhouse, where the horses the men had ridden in on were standing with heaving flanks.

'That big bay looks like Ben Murdock's mount,' he declared. 'It fooled me for a moment. I thought it was Ben riding in. We sent a man over to Circle M to fetch him.'

'That's what Charlene thought,' Hart said. 'Let's go take a look at the animal.'

'I sent Frank Webber to tell Ben what had happened here,' Benteen said. 'So why hasn't he come back? I told him to push it. He should have showed up again an hour ago.'

They walked on across the yard and Roper caught hold of the reins of the bay. The animal was nervous, rolling its eyes and cavorting, and the cowpuncher soothed it gently. Benteen walked around the animal, patting its flanks and stroking its nose.

'If this ain't Ben Murdock's horse then I'm a monkey's uncle,' he said. 'Look at the black spots on its muzzle. Ben's horse is marked like that. And this bald patch on the left side of its neck. That clinches it for me. This is Ben's horse, for sure.'

'So what is a stranger doing on it, riding in here and shooting up the place?' Roper demanded.

'I hesitate to put my tongue to the answer.' Benteen shook his head.

'I'll do more than voice it,' Hart said harshly. 'I'll back-track the horse until I find Ben Murdock. I think he was riding here after getting word about

Art, and someone ambushed him. Perhaps that was part of the plan.'

'I don't think he would have ridden here alone,' Benteen mused. 'He never leaves the Circle M without Panhandle Harper siding him.'

'So where is Panhandle?' Roper asked. 'He ain't a man to get bushwhacked.'

'You can't do anything about a bullet in the back, no matter how good you are.' Benteen shook his head. 'Joe, you better ride with Hart. He's a stranger here and will need someone to show him around.'

Hart bent to study the hoof prints of the bay before turning to go back to the house for his horse. Charlene was standing just inside the doorway, peering out from behind a door post.

'Benteen seems to think that bay is your uncle's horse,' Hart said. 'I'm riding out with Joe Roper to check its back trail.'

'Do you think Ben is dead?'

'I never jump to conclusions.' Hart shook his head. 'I hope to find him alive.'

'You'll come back and let us know if anything bad has happened to him, won't you?' she asked.

'You can count on it.' Hart stepped up into his saddle and rode out.

Roper joined him and they headed up the valley. Hart's keen gaze was checking out the tracks of the four horses that had carried the raiders in. They passed the incoming herd and continued, riding into the cold, gusty wind.

Hart's eyes were watering, and he blinked rapidly

to clear them. He needed to be at a high point of alertness in this deadly game. The grey sky was heavy with racing clouds, and his experience indicated that snow could not far away. He knew from bitter experience that when the snow came his job would be almost impossible to pursue. Tracks would be wiped out; movement almost non-existent. He struggled against impatience and maintained his high peak of alertness, for any lapse could be punished by death.

Two hours later they were clear of the valley and riding into the high, broken ground that formed the base of the Coulee Hills. The tracks continued, and Hart began to experience a prickly sensation between his shoulder blades. He glanced at Roper, who was hunched in his saddle, his neckerchief up over his nose and his hat brim pulled low over his eyes.

'I think we're being followed,' Hart called, his voice buffeted by the wind. 'Ride on slow while I drop back to check.'

Roper nodded and continued. Hart turned aside the instant he crossed a rise and was out of sight of anyone on his back trail. He trailed his reins, aware that his horse would not stray a step, and drew his Winchester from its boot. He dropped to the ground and crawled back up the rise to the crest, removing his hat before taking a look over the rough ground they had already traversed. He was thankful to have his back to the wind, and settled down to watch the desolate ground.

Within minutes he caught a movement among a pile of rocks, and slipped the glove off his right hand.

Two riders emerged from cover, moving slowly, heads bent forward as they checked tracks. They came straight towards the spot where Hart was waiting, and he prepared for action. When they were barely ten feet from him, he rose up suddenly, his Winchester covering them. Both men reined in quickly, startled by his unexpected appearance. The one on the right reached to his hip for a pistol; the other lifted a rifle lying across his thighs.

'Hold it right there!' Hart called. 'I'm a Texas Ranger.'

The man who was reaching for his pistol froze under the menace of Hart's rifle, and then lifted his hands wide of his body. The one with the rifle kept moving, intent on shooting. Hart fired a single shot that thumped into the man's chest. The sound of the shot was shredded and dissipated by the powerful wind. It sounded puny, somehow ineffective, but the result was normal. The man tumbled out of his saddle and lay motionless on the cold ground while his horse lowered its head and began to graze as if nothing had happened.

'Who are you and what's your business?' Hart demanded. The muzzle of his rifle was centred unwaveringly on the man's breastbone.

'I'm Jake Kenney. I got a farm up there in the hills. Me and Dave Latter were riding home after a day in Ashville.'

'So why did you start to draw on me?'

'I don't know about Dave, but I reckoned you was one of those troublemakers we got around here.'

Hart considered and discounted that. 'I told you I'm a Ranger. Were you with Pat Gedge at the JB ranch this morning?'

Kenney shook his head. 'We ain't mixed up in that business.'

'What business?'

'Gedge is pushing for trouble with the cattlemen. He wants to move in among them and raise trouble.'

'Is that a fact? It sounds like Gedge is a man keen on committing suicide. No one in his right mind would go up against the two big Murdock spreads. Get rid of your weapon and then check on Latter. Don't try to get smart or you'll wind up dead. In case you weren't with Gedge this morning and saw me, I'll tell you again that I'm Mike Hart, Texas Ranger.'

'I'm a law-abiding man,' Kenney said, disarming himself. 'You won't get any trouble from me.'

Hart stood motionless while Kenney dismounted and bent over Latter. The farmer straightened immediately and looked up at Hart.

'He's dead,' he said in a shocked tone.

'That's what happens when men go out to make trouble. If you pull a gun you better be sure you can beat the man you're facing. So why were you trailing me?'

'We weren't. I told you, we were on our way home from Ashville.'

'That won't wash. I saw you watching tracks, and Latter had his rifle across his saddle, ready for trouble. I think you and some other farmers ambushed Ben Murdock a short time ago, and you were out to

60

raise hell against anyone who showed up. Anyway, that don't matter right now. Get back in your saddle and ride ahead of me. I'm on my way to Circle M. Do you know where that is?'

'Yeah.'

'Well make for it, and don't get any ideas about outsmarting me.'

Kenney climbed back into his saddle and Hart mounted. They rode north, with Hart a few yards behind the farmer. Presently, Hart saw a rider coming towards them, and called for Kenney to halt. The next moment Joe Roper confronted them.

'I heard the shot,' Roper said. 'Did you kill someone?'

'I usually do when I fire my pistol,' Hart replied grimly. 'This time it was a farmer named Latter. This is his pard, Jake Kenney. They were tracking us, and Latter reckoned to shoot me.'

'I found Ben Murdock and Panhandle Harper up ahead.' Roper spoke jerkily. 'They're both dead. Someone ambushed them – filled them full of lead. Frank Webber is with them. He's our man, sent to tell Ben about Art being shot. There'll be hell to pay over this.'

Hart considered the news. He had suspected from the start, when he saw O'Hara tied to the hitch rack in Ashville, that he was late upon the scene. Events were evolving fast, and he had to get in, locate the background facts, and then start his grim business of knocking out the bad men before too many innocents were killed.

'Did you check the tracks at the scene?' Hart asked.

'No. I rode in close enough to check the bodies, but I didn't want to muss up any tracks.'

'Let's get on. Watch Kenney for me, Joe. We'll take him on to Circle M.'

'Don't hand me over to any cattlemen,' Kenney said nervously. 'I told you I ain't mixed up in this trouble. I got a wife and two kids at home. I told Gedge I didn't want anything to do with his scheme.'

They went on, and Hart moved in alone when he saw the three bodies sprawled on the ground. He shook his head sadly when he recognized Ben Murdock's big figure, and recalled the man's attitude in town. Then he got down to business. He stood and looked around, reading what had occurred from the many hoof prints in the dust.

'There were six men in the ambush party,' he told Roper. 'Three of them dismounted there and climbed into the saddles of the men they had killed. Four rode on to A Bar M to attack the place. You know what happened there. Perhaps you'll ride on to Circle M, Joe, and acquaint them with this news. Then you better go back to A Bar M and tell Miss Murdock that her uncle is dead.'

'What are you going to do?' Roper asked. 'And what do I do with Kenney? If I take him into Circle M, and they figure that farmers killed their boss, Kenney is gonna be crow-bait mighty quick. Wouldn't it be better if you took him with you? He might be able to help you if you come up against farmers.'

62

'I want to know where the ambush party came from,' Hart said. 'I'll back-track them until I find out.' He glanced at the shocked face of Jake Kenney. 'I'll take you at your word for now, Kenney, so you can go. My advice to you is, go home and stay there until this trouble is over.'

'I'll do that.' Kenney turned his horse instantly and rode off.

Roper shook his head. 'I wouldn't have turned him loose,' he said. 'If he is mixed up in this then he'll ride straight to Gedge and warn him.'

'I hope he will,' Hart replied, 'because I'm gonna be sitting on his tail all the way. See you later, Joe. I'll need to come back to A Bar M later. I'll take the body of that man who shot Art Murdock into town and try to get him identified.'

They parted then, and Hart tracked Kenney into the gathering gloom of late afternoon. The farmer rode at a fast pace and never once checked his back trail. Hart stayed far enough back to remain unnoticed, and was intrigued when Kenney suddenly turned east and rode into a maze of rocks in a large stretch of broken ground.

Hart maintained his position behind Kenney, and wondered where the farmer was heading. He knew from looking at the map in Buckbee's office that the farming section was not in this direction. Miles slipped by, and daylight began to fade. Hart dared not close in, but knew he would lose Kenney if he stayed back, for he would have to halt when the light became too bad, which meant spending an uncomfortable night in this lonely wasteland, with more tracking in the morning.

Darkness fell without warning. The sun, hidden by dense clouds, had passed behind a distant hill. Hart dismounted and patted his horse. He made camp, ensured that the animal was sheltered from the wind, and then ate cold food. He was about to turn in when his keen nose caught the tang of wood smoke on the wind, and he stood for some moments in the darkness, sniffing like an animal scenting prey.

It might be Jake Kenney camping for the night, but Hart knew he could not accept that without checking. He heaved a sigh and took his rifle, then moved out of camp, heading straight into the wind and the giveaway smell of smoke.

He moved silently, feeling his way and taking his time, unable to see to any great distance. But the smell of smoke grew stronger as he continued and he tensed for action. He took another cautious step forward into the darkness and came up against a large rock. Moving to the right of the obstruction, his tentative foot lost contact with the hard ground and he pitched sideways, unbalanced by the unexpected movement. He fell sideways and downwards, accompanied by a shower of small rocks and stones, and then plunged into a ravine about twelve feet deep.

Fortunately, he landed on his left shoulder on a slope and broke his fall before rolling another six feet. He was semi-stunned, and lay for a moment listening to the shower of stones settling around him. He sat up, still grasping his rifle in his left hand. The wind was boring down the ravine, channelled by its containing walls, and the smell of smoke was even stronger.

Hart got to his feet. He had collected several bruises in his unexpected descent but counted himself lucky. He followed the ravine through blackness so complete he could have carved his initials on it. His ears were strained to pick up sounds, but the wind moaning through the ravine cloaked any other sound, including his own movements.

A flickering light ahead warned him of company, and he halted and canted his head to pick up noise. Somehow, he did not think it would be Jake Kenney. He heard a horse stamp, its shod hoof clashing against rock. Then a voice sounded, harsh and echoing.

'Taco, take a look down the ravine and check it out. I got a nasty feeling we're not alone.'

'You're getting nervy in your old age, Trace.' A voice laughed raucously. 'There ain't anybody out there on a night like this.'

'Just do like I tell you, huh? I ain't got to this age by taking any chances. You know what my hunches are like. And Kenney said there's a Ranger in the county.'

'I think it's about time we quit this game. It was OK while the law was out of it, but we don't need to tangle with Rangers. Kill one of them and the rest won't stop until they nail you.'

Hart found a large rock at the side of the ravine and crawled behind it, his mind flitting over the snatch of conversation. He heard boots grating on rock as the man called Taco came down the ravine. Taco, he thought; an unusual nickname, but one he had heard before – Taco Tate was one of the Bascombe gang of bank robbers. And Trace could be no other than Trace Bascombe, the gang leader.

Hardly able to believe his luck, Hart waited stolidly for the outlaw to pass along the ravine. He heard the man curse as he stumbled on a loose stone, and then he passed Hart's position and silence followed. Hart remained motionless, his muscles cramping in the cold air, but he dared not move, and after a timeless period he heard Taco returning.

'Nothing doing down there,' the outlaw reported when he reached the blazing fire. 'You're getting jumpy, Trace.'

'Mebbe so. All the same, we're moving out in the morning. I never ignore my hunches.'

'Are we quitting this game? It's about time we went back to our own business.'

'We'll go when I've got what we were promised. I ain't set eyes on that piker Crane in a couple of weeks. He's good at throwing out his orders, but he sure don't like paying for what we do. And where in hell have Carver and Eke got to? They were supposed to be back here before dark.'

Silence fell, and Hart considered what had been said. He had stumbled upon an outlaw camp, thanks to Jake Kenney, and only two members of the gang were here. Hart felt a tingling behind his breast-bone. This was a heaven-sent opportunity to take advantage of the situation. He had even heard Bascombe mention Crane.

He waited in cover, his patience inexhaustible, like a hungry predator waiting to pounce on its prey. He could see the gleam of the camp-fire and smell the pungent tang that had attracted him in the first place. This was a breakthrough, and he could do no other than play the hand that fate had thrust upon him. The question of the outlaws had lain in the back of his mind from the moment he arrived in Ashville, for they were professional outlaws and he needed to put them away before they learned of his presence. But Kenney had told Bascombe a Ranger was here and in action, and he had to act while the initiative was his.

An hour passed and Hart did not move. He was lying on his left side behind a large rock. Sharp pieces of stone were digging into his thigh; a large piece pressing into his ribs, but he dared not move. He needed to wait until the two outlaws were asleep before closing in. By raising his head slightly, he could see the glow of the fire, and noted that its brightness was fading. There was no more talking between the outlaws, and he wondered if both were asleep. They were desperate men well used to the back trails, and he fancied one of them might be on guard.

Another hour slid silently into the past before Hart decided to move. Lying on the cold, uneven ground had enabled a chill to seep into his body from the obdurate rock. He was shivering with cold, his teeth chattering convulsively, and was aware that at the moment he was in no fit condition to tackle Bascombe and Tate. He edged forward very slowly, an inch or two at a time, flexing his fingers to encourage his circulation to return to normal.

The glow of the fire revealed something of its immediate surroundings. It was positioned in the mouth of a small cave in a wall of rock that reared up into the impenetrable darkness above. Hart wondered where the outlaws' horses were hitched. No outlaw of Bascombe's calibre would be far from his only means of escape. Were the animals in the cave?

Hart decided to wait until daylight before tackling Bascombe. He did not know how many men were holed up in the cave. He had heard two talking, but he could not assume there were no more. He eased to the right, able to see that the ravine twisted in that direction to pass along in front of the high rock wall containing the cave.

A smaller cave thirty yards from the one Bascombe was occupying showed as a slighter darker shadow in the black night. Hart eased towards it like an animal seeking its lair. He needed to get under cover and, such was the situation, he could not afford to be choosy.

Silence and darkness were intense, and the slight noises he made seemed like thunderclaps in Hart's ears, but the outlaws gave no indication of alarm, and Hart was relieved when he finally lay inside the cave. He hunched down just inside the entrance, pulled his thick coat more closely around his body, and forced himself to wait out the long night.

He fell asleep some time after midnight, and lay as dead for hours, exhausted by the events of the previous day, and then awoke suddenly, half-frozen and badly cramped. He sensed that all was not well, and reached for his holstered gun as he sat up, seeing immediately a man crouching nearby, covering him with a levelled pistol in his hand.

FIVE

'You were sleeping so peacefully it was a shame to wake you,' the man said, waggling his pistol. 'Who are you and what the hell are you doing here?'

Hart glanced around, and his teeth clicked together in exasperation. What he had thought was a cave was nothing more than a tunnel through the rock. He could see grey daylight showing at the far end.

'I reckoned this was a cave like the one Trace is in,' he said.

'Nope. It leads into the valley where the rest of us have to sleep. Didn't Trace tell you to come through? Where's your horse?'

'I left it back down the ravine. It was dark when I got here last night, and I didn't want to rouse the whole camp.'

'And you snuck in here till morning, huh? And Trace don't know you came in? Heck, he must be getting old. Nobody could have got past him in the old days. Who are you, anyway? I ain't seen you around before. That's the trouble with this job – too many strange faces showing up all the time. If they ain't farmers then they're rustlers. If Trace ain't careful he'll have the law turning up next.'

'I'm Mike Hart. Crane sent me.' Hart was recalling what he had overheard Bascombe and Tate saying the night before.

'Well, you're plumb unlucky. Trace and Taco planned to ride out before daylight this morning. I was on my way to see if they'd left when I found you. They're going to gee-up Gedge a little. He's been dragging his feet lately. Give me Crane's message and I'll see it gets to Trace when he comes back. I'm Emmet Eke. I run the gang when Trace ain't around. We're gonna clean up good when everything falls into place.'

'Crane said to lay off A Bar M until he knows whether Art Murdock is gonna die.' Hart got to his feet and Eke holstered his gun. 'Ben Murdock is dead, so the rustlers will move in on Circle M today and empty the range.'

'There's a Ranger showed up, I hear,' Eke said. 'One of our boys was in Ashville when he came in — saw him kill Kenyon and down two others. Something will have to be done about him before he starts cutting loose. Do you want some grub before you pull out?'

'No thanks. I got to head back to town. See you around.'

'So long,' Eke replied.

Hart saw two men approaching from along the tunnel and turned away. He started out of the tunnel mouth, and then stopped short, for a man stepped in front of him from the right with a levelled pistol in his hand.

'Hold it right there,' the newcomer rasped. 'You ain't going any place.'

'What took you so long?' Eke complained, drawing his pistol again. 'I ran out of things to say, and he certainly gave me the lowdown on what's going on around here. He told me things I didn't know had happened. Is he the Ranger Bob was talking about?'

'Yeah. It's him. I saw him shooting the lights outa Crane's men in the saloon. They said Kenyon was faster'n most, but this guy left him standing, and hit him dead centre. Take his gun, Eke, before he starts using it.'

'You get it, Snap. I'll cover him.' Eke grinned. 'Watch he doesn't bite you.'

'Yeah? Well you should have seen him in town. I've been around guns all my life but I never saw a draw like his. He must have been born with it.'

The two men approaching from along the tunnel came abreast of Eke and paused.

'He's the Ranger,' said one of them.

'So let's take him into the hideout and hold him until Trace gets back,' Eke replied.

Hart was motionless and outwardly calm although his mind seethed with anticipation. All four men were holding guns which were covering him, and he was aware that he did not have a chance of beating them. He also knew that if they disarmed him his chances would drop to less than zero.

'Get your hands up, and don't even blink, Ranger,' Eke grated, his manner suddenly grim. 'I told you to take his gun, Snap. What in hell are you waiting for?'

Hart raised his hands shoulder high, resignation showing on his face, and Snap moved a step nearer, reaching out with his left hand to snatch Hart's pistol from its holster while his right hand aimed his Colt at Hart's chest. In doing so he inadvertently stepped between Hart and Eke, and Hart sent his left hand down in a circular movement, like trying to catch a fly on the wing. His cupped hand struck Snap's gun hand and pushed it aside so fast that when Snap triggered a shot it went wide. At the same time, Hart lifted his knee to Snap's belly. He drew his own pistol as he hurled himself to his left, dropping to the rock floor and bringing his deadly gun into action.

Snap went down and rolled, trying desperately to line up his pistol on Hart's fast-moving figure, and Hart shot him in the chest. Guns thundered in the close confines of the tunnel. Eke was lunging to his right, trying to get a clear shot at Hart. The other two outlaws were separating and bringing weapons into play, shooting wildly.

Hart triggered his pistol as gunsmoke flared. His second shot took Eke in the throat, and he rolled away out of the mouth of the tunnel as the remaining two outlaws finally got his position bracketed. Six-guns crashed and bullets whined in ricochet from the rock walls. Hart felt a blow like the kick of a mule hip-high on his right side but felt no pain, and realized that a bullet had struck his holster. His pistol bucked in his hand and one of the two remaining outlaws dropped his gun and jack-knifed to the rocky floor of the tunnel.

Diving and rolling to his left, Hart dropped into the cover of a jumble of rocks lying outside the tunnel mouth. He got to his feet and ran swiftly along the ravine, and realized that he had passed the gully he had originally fallen into the night before, which led back to his waiting horse. When he ran by the cave where Bascombe and Taco Tate had spent the night, there was no time to retrace his steps and he kept moving along another gully that bore the imprints here and there of hoofs.

Hart saw the black mouth of yet another cave in the rock wall, some forty feet beyond the one Bascombe had used. He ducked into it, dropped flat and squirmed around to await pursuit. His ears were ringing from the shock of the shooting, and he waited until all echoes had faded before easing forward until he could look back along the rocky cut he had traversed.

There was no sign of pursuit, and he was aware that only one of the four outlaws who had accosted him was unwounded. He reloaded his pistol, eased forward out of the cave, and retraced his steps to the tunnel. Peering inside, he found Eke and another outlaw lying dead, and saw the unwounded outlaw in the act of helping the wounded Snap out of the other end of the tunnel.

Hart paused only to collect his rifle, which was lying where he had put it the night before, and then hurried in pursuit. He ran along the tunnel, and emerged to find himself on the brink of a narrow valley. He paused, checking his rifle while he looked across the valley. There were several figures moving around a shack in the middle distance — seven, Hart counted quickly. A number of horses were milling around in a small corral behind the shack, and the unwounded outlaw, burdened with Snap, was hurrying in a shambling run down a shale slope in front of the tunnel mouth.

It was then that Hart heard the clatter of hoofs on rock coming from behind him, and whirled to see the first of several riders entering the tunnel from the outside. He ducked, and then dropped into cover as a gun hammered. A slug struck the ground just in front of him and whined by his right ear as it ricocheted off an obdurate rock. He returned fire, and the foremost rider vacated his saddle with a cry of anguish that was all but obliterated by the thunderous report of the shot. The horse came on, and Hart moved aside as it passed him and plunged recklessly down the slope into the valley.

The other riders reined up outside the tunnel, dismounted, and came forward on foot. A volley of shots hammered and Hart moved out of the tunnel mouth, aware that he was trapped. A glance into the valley revealed that the outlaws around the shack were now hurrying forward to join in the fight.

Hart wondered if he had come to the end of his trail. He had nowhere to go, and the odds were greater than any he had faced in his long career, but even as the thought crossed his mind he was looking for the best possible spot from which to conduct his defence. He was outnumbered by about fifteen to one, but those opposing him — outlaws and saddle scum – were his legal prey, and he would not hesitate to take them on. They would give him no quarter, and he wanted none. He would fight them to the death.

He heard boots crashing on the rock floor of the tunnel as the dismounted riders came in a rush to swamp his resistance, and raised himself, despite the slugs coming in his direction, to empty his pistol into the confined space. His shots tore through flesh and stopped the charge in its tracks. He moved then, retiring from the tunnel, and dropped into a small depression that was half-hidden by brush. He waited, reloading his pistol, his gaze on the tunnel and, moments later, when he spotted movement there, holstered his pistol and tossed three rifle slugs into its blackness. Echoes tore away across the valley.

He moved again, this time looking for the men approaching from the shack. He did not want a fight with attackers coming from two directions, and real-ized that his best tactic would be to fire and move while he could. A head appeared in the mouth of the tunnel, rising up cautiously, and Hart sent a slug at it. He turned his head to look towards the shack, and decided to move before he was pinned down in one spot.

Hart was sweating despite the cold wind tearing at him, but there was a coldness inside him that had nothing to do with the weather. Shooting started again, this time coming from the direction of the shack, and he hunched down, waiting for sight of his adversaries. They were closing in like a wolf pack. He could hear the furtive sounds of their concerted movements through the brush.

If he could get out of the valley and find his waiting horse he would have a chance. The thought crossed his mind. The odds against him at the moment were too great, and he would be a fool to stay and fight to the death. He had a job to do, and dying uselessly in this wilderness was not a part of it. He moved to his left, making a circular approach to the tunnel he had vacated. That way lay survival, if he could draw out or kill the men inside it.

He saw a figure moving into view in the tunnel but did not shoot and kept easing slowly to his left. The figure ducked, expecting to draw fire, and then reappeared when nothing happened. The next moment three men stood in the mouth of the tunnel, guns held ready, and Hart was tempted to shoot at them but wisely refrained. He could hear the outlaws getting closer from the direction of the shack and knew it was time for flight rather than action. He slid into a long depression that angled away to the left and kept moving, drawing well away from his earlier position.

'What in hell is going on here?' yelled one of the men now standing in the mouth of the tunnel. 'What's all the shooting about? Who was tossing lead at us?'

The outlaw who had led the wounded Snap out of the tunnel raised himself up briefly and replied, 'A Texas Ranger showed up last night. Four of us tried to nail him but he beat us to it. He's hell on wheels! You better come in and help us pick him off.'

Hart smiled grimly and moved further to his left. The trio in the tunnel mouth left their cover and walked steadily towards the group coming from the shack. They passed Hart's position, and he immediately eased forward to the shale slope leading up to the tunnel mouth. When the newcomers reached a spot where they shielded Hart from the view of those coming from the shack, he sprang up and ran up the slope to the tunnel mouth.

Shouts and then shots rang out when he was spotted. He heard slugs crackling close by but it was panic-shooting, and he flung himself headlong into the tunnel before the outlaws could recover from their surprise. Twisting around, he lifted his rifle and cut loose at the half-dozen men he could see standing in the open and shooting at him. Three of them fell to his fire before the rest realized the danger of exposing themselves and disappeared into the brush.

Hart grinned as he stopped shooting. Now the boot was on the other foot. He was in cover and the opposition was out in the open. But he had no desire to continue this fight. He needed to get on with his investigation and collect evidence against the leaders who had organized the lawlessness. He backed away and left the tunnel to return to his horse, aware that Trace Bascombe was no longer here but could return at any time with others.

He was not displeased with the way the fight had turned out. No doubt the surviving outlaws would flee the hideout, and Hart would have been much happier wiping them out completely, but he had thrown a scare into them as well as cutting down their numbers, and left the ravine to return to the spot where his horse was waiting.

He checked out the surroundings before moving in close, and found the campsite as he had left it. He took care of his horse and ate cold food before breaking camp and moving out on his original course. He knew that Jake Kenney had visited Bascombe and warned the outlaw that a Ranger was in the county. He had heard Bascombe talk of Bart Crane, which tied them neatly together, but he needed proof of the situation that existed before Captain Buckbee would be halfway satisfied. He decided to visit Gedge and, with a little luck, take the farmer into custody and sweat the truth out of him.

The wind blew into his face with monotonous tenacity. He watched his surroundings closely as he continued, aware that somewhere to his left was the Circle M ranch, and he wondered at the changes that would be wrought on this part of the range by the death of Ben Murdock.

Hart angled more to the north-west. He could see the Coulee Hills rearing up ahead and wondered about the farming community. Most of the farmers, he knew, were honest and God-fearing, wanting nothing more than to be left alone to follow their livelihood. Men like Gedge were not true farmers, and would turn on whoever did not follow the crooked policy that was in force.

That afternoon found Hart entering the foothills that were rising up and altering the nature of the country. When he came across the nearest farm he sat and studied the peaceful scene. There was a big yard in front of a large cabin. Chickens were scratching in the dirt, pigs rooting around, and there was a rough pasture with a dozen milk cows grazing in it. He saw a woman emerge from a barn and walk towards the cabin. She glanced in his direction, and was galvanized by the sight of him into running back to the barn.

Hart gigged his mount and went forward to the yard. A man emerged from the barn toting a shotgun, and paused in the doorway to watch his approach. Hart rode up and reined in.

'Howdy,' he greeted. 'I'm looking for Pat Gedge. Can you point me in his direction?'

The farmer, a man in his fifties, regarded him with suspicion. He held his shotgun across the front of his body, the twin muzzles pointing skywards.

'I guess I could tell you, but that depends on what you want him for.'

'I saw him this morning talking to Mrs Baines at the JB ranch. We didn't get a chance to say much, so I thought I'd look him up. Where at is his farm?'

'Beyond that tall hill over yonder.' The farmer pointed with his shotgun. 'Follow that path over there and it'll bring you right into Gedge's yard. He

80

rode past here yesterday. I ain't seen him today. But he ain't long at his farm these days, and that's why he's got Jenson and Harrap running the place. You're welcome to 'light and eat if you've a mind to.'

'Thanks, but I need to push on. There ain't a lot of daylight left and I got things to do.'

'Snow will be flying in less than a week. Better get your chores done by then.'

Hart nodded and reined away. He skirted the fields and rode on without looking back, pushing his horse into a canter. The nature of the countryside had changed completely. Now he was riding through fields that still bore signs of their last crops. There were hay and straw stacks containing winter food and fodder, and when he came to a bobwire fence with a gate in it he considered it for a moment before riding through. Wire was the main cause of trouble between farmers and cattlemen. It had started range wars in the past, and would do so again.

It was late afternoon when Hart jogged around a tall hill and spotted a large farm in the near distance. He rode into the yard and came immediately under the guns of two men standing in front of a big cabin. They were dressed as farmers, but there all similarities ended. Hart could tell at a glance that they were more at home with guns in their hands than farming implements. Before he reached the cabin, one of the men called to him.

'This is private property and strangers ain't welcome. Turn around and ride out or you'll get a bellyful of buckshot.'

'Is this Pat Gedge's farm?' Hart did not stop moving forward until he was within six feet of the two men. He gazed at them steadily.

'Who wants to know?' demanded the second man. His bearded face was set in harsh lines and his eyes held a fierce glitter that warned Hart there could be trouble.

'I've got business with Gedge,' he replied.

'Well he ain't here.'

'You're Jenson and Harrap, huh?' Hart nodded. He sat tall in the saddle, quite motionless, holding his reins in his left hand while his right hand lay on his thigh just in front of his holstered pistol. 'Which of you is Jenson?'

'That ain't none of your business. You were told to get outa here, so move it.'

'I heard that farmers are hospitable,' Hart observed.

'We got trouble in these parts so callers ain't welcome.'

'Any idea where Gedge is? He'll be concerned that he missed me.'

'He rode out to Elm Ridge this morning. I reckon he won't be back inside of two days. You've had your ride for nothing.'

'Mind if I water my horse?' Hart asked.

'Help yourself, and then ride on. You been here too long already.'

Hart reined to the left and rode across to a well. He dismounted and drew up a bucket of water. As his mount drank its fill, Hart glanced over to the cabin to see both men still standing motionless, watching him closely. He touched a forefinger to the brim of his Stetson, swung into his saddle, and trotted away. The moment he was out of sight of the house he reined in, dismounted, and sneaked back to view the cabin. When he was able to see it he found both men gone from sight.

Moments later the farmer with the beard drove out of the barn in a buggy and headed north without looking around. Hart climbed back into his saddle and followed at a distance. He pulled his neckerchief up over his mouth and nose and eased his hat brim down a fraction to protect his eyes.

For an hour the buggy moved steadily along the trail, and Hart began to think night would come before his quarry reached his destination. The buggy ascended a sharp rise and then vanished as if it had fallen into a ravine. Hart reached the top of the rise and saw a farm way down the reverse slope. He watched the buggy enter the yard and stop in front of a cabin.

There were at least ten horses standing in the yard, and Hart eased back off the skyline before dismounting and going forward to see what was afoot. He saw four men climbing into their saddles, and the next instant they were flogging their mounts and coming out of the yard as if pursued by a devil. Hart narrowed his eyes as he watched, and then stark realization hit him. They were coming for him.

He swung into his saddle and paused to look back at the farm. There was no doubt the four riders were after him. One of them fired a pistol, and Hart heard the crackle of the bullet as it passed by his right ear. He set spurs into the flanks of his horse and moved out of view, accompanied by a burst of shooting that set echoes hammering across the desolate land.

SIX

Hart sought cover and turned off the trail into deep brush. He had barely found a suitable place to hide when he heard the approach of the four riders. They came at a gallop, guns in their hands, and he drew his pistol as they neared his position. He was relieved when they continued along the trail, not looking left or right, and watched them gallop on out of sight along his back trail. He was aware that they would be returning when they realized he had turned off, and went deeper into the brush circling around the farm, wanting to get into a position beyond it. He was intrigued by the gathering at the farm, and wondered at its significance.

Shadows were beginning to creep across the land, filling in the depressions and cutting down range of vision. Hart rode where he could and walked his horse when the brush was not tall enough to conceal him. He found a gully to the rear of the cabin and tethered his horse in its depths. Taking his rifle, he moved forward grimly, ready to continue his deadly work.

He reached the back of the cabin without incident and stood within its shadow. A lamp was burning in the small building, and he searched for a chink in the wall to take a look inside, but there was no crack or knot-hole that he could use. He inched along the back wall to the right-hand back corner, hoping to be able to look through a window. The side wall was blank, and he moved along it to the front corner.

One of the dozen waiting horses sensed him and whickered softly to announce his presence. He heard voices inside the cabin but could not make out what was being said. Peering around the corner, he saw half-a-dozen men grouped around the doorway, smoking and chatting, and Hart wondered who they were.

He waited patiently, listening to the conversation, but heard nothing of interest. Then a loud voice cut through the chat.

'Mount up, men. We're heading out. Let's go get those Circle M cows.'

Hart eased back slightly as the men made a concerted move to their waiting horses, and there was a tight smile on his lips as he considered. These men were rustlers. He waited until they had ridden out and then moved along the front wall of the cabin to a window at the left of the door. Risking a look inside the building, he saw Pat Gedge seated at a table, engaged in conversation with another man.

'That's the way of it,' Gedge was saying. 'We've got to stick together now. That Ranger is gonna make the job more difficult. I'll see Crane and ask him to get the outlaws to handle the Ranger. We're not gunnies, and Crane will have to give us some protection. Things are coming to a head now, and we need a clear trail to pull it all together.'

'Where is Crane?' the other man demanded. 'He's never around when you want him. He's all right throwing out orders, but when it comes to doing something important, he's not here.'

'He pays others to take the risks,' Gedge said. 'It'll all be over shortly. With the Murdocks dead and gone there'll be no one to stand in our way. We'll have the best farms in the county, and Crane will be ranching on the rest of the range.'

'I heard Ben Murdock was killed yesterday, but what about Art? He was only wounded. Is he gonna be taken care of?'

'He'll be dead before morning. Four of the men are riding into A Bar M now to finish him off.'

'I thought they went after that Ranger.'

'They'll get him if they see him, but they've got a special chore to handle.'

Hart clenched his teeth at the harsh words, and moved out immediately. He eased away from the cabin and went back to his horse. Within minutes he was clear of the farm and galloping along the trail back the way he had come. His perfect sense of direction stood him in good stead and he rode unerringly towards A Bar M.

It was late when he saw lights ahead, and slowed, wondering what kind of a reception he would receive. The four riders who passed him back at the farm had got a good head start, and he wondered where they were. But the ranch seemed quiet, and he hoped he was in time to prevent the further attempt on Art Murdock's life.

He rode in openly, certain that the crew would be on their guard, and a harsh voice challenged him as he reached the yard.

'You're covered on two sides. Stop and throw up your hands.'

Hart obeyed, and the shadows split as a dark figure came forward.

'I'm Mike Hart, Texas Ranger. Has there been any trouble here since I left yesterday?'

'Heck, I've been wondering about you. I'm Joe Roper. We rode out together to Circle M.'

Roper lowered his rifle and Hart stepped down from his saddle, trailing his reins.

'It's been quiet since I got back last night,' Roper informed him. 'Too quiet, I think.'

'How's Art Murdock doing?'

'He's hanging on, Doc says.'

'Four men were heading this way earlier,' Hart said, 'coming to kill Art, so be ready for anything, Joe. I'll go up to the house and warn them.'

Hart climbed back into his saddle and rode across the yard to where a light showed in a front window of the ranch house. He dismounted wearily, staggering slightly as he wrapped his reins around the hitch rack in front of the porch. A figure moved forward from the dense shadows and became silhouetted against the yellow light emanating from a nearby window.

'Keep in the shadows,' Hart rapped, and then recognized Charlene Murdock's slim figure and eased his tone slightly. 'It's not safe out here, Miss Murdock.'

'Mister Hart! I've been worried about you. Joe came back last night with the news of my uncle's death, and said you had gone off following a trail.'

'How is your father?'

'Holding his own, so Doc Chilvers says. The ranch is like a fort at the moment, but no one knows exactly what to do. The crew wanted to go out looking for the gang responsible for the trouble, but Hemp said we should wait until you got back. He wouldn't let anyone leave the spread, and thinks an attack is imminent.'

'He could be right.' Hart stepped on to the porch and placed his back to the front wall of the house while he gazed around into the shadows. 'I know four men are on their way here to kill your father. They should be very close now, waiting to strike. Where is Benteen?'

'He's out there somewhere. We have guards out, and I don't think any raiders could get past them. I've been stuck in the house all day, and came out for a breath of fresh air.'

Charlene moved to the door of the house as she spoke, and Hart followed her closely.

'I also heard that the Circle M herd will be rustled tonight,' Hart said. 'I came straight here because your father's life is more important than cattle.'

'You saw Uncle Ben dead on the trail, didn't you?'

Worry etched every line in the girl's face. 'I haven't told my father yet. It might be too much for him. He's got an uphill fight to survive. Have you any idea who is back of this trouble?'

'Yes. But knowing isn't enough. I have to catch up with them. I think I'll spend the rest of the night here in case there's another attempt made against your father. Tomorrow I'll ride over to Circle M, and if the herd has been rustled I'll go after the thieves.'

'Have you eaten at all?' she queried. 'Can I get you anything?'

'I don't get a chance to eat much when I'm about my business.' Hart smiled ruefully. 'I could sure do with something hot, even if it's only coffee.'

'Come into the kitchen and I'll get you a meal.'

'Thank you.' Hart followed her through the lower rooms of the house and sat down at the big table in the kitchen. He watched Charlene moving around, and presently the smell of cooking food pervaded his nostrils and he realized just how hungry he was.

He was halfway through eating the meal the girl prepared for him when Hemp Benteen came into the kitchen. The foreman was looking weary, and sat down opposite Hart and had a cup of coffee. Hart gave a brief account of his actions over the past twenty-four hours and Benteen shook his head.

'I'd like for us to gather the crew and ride out after these bad men once for all,' he said harshly.

'I think there's gonna be an attempt made against your boss between now and the morning,' Hart replied. 'You've got to guard against that. I want to go over to Circle M and alert the crew about rustlers. The thieves are planning to strike tonight.'

'You've been real busy if you learned all this since you rode out yesterday,' Benteen said, shaking his head.

'It doesn't usually take long to find out who's back of any trouble. The problem comes in trying to bring the guilty to justice. Someone has gathered together a pretty big bunch of bad men to pull off this job, and they've gotten themselves well organized.'

Hart finished his meal and felt better for it. He thanked the girl and prepared to leave. Repeating his warning of trouble coming to them, he was satisfied that Benteen could handle the chore and left quickly. Benteen saw him out to the porch, and Hart requested a fresh horse. He was given a good replacement, and Benteen walked to the gate with him.

'Can you find your way to Circle M in the dark?' Benteen asked.

'Can you spare a rider to show me the way?'

'Sure, Joe will go along with you. I got enough men around here to take care of the place. There are guards watching all approaches. Joe, fetch your horse and go with Hart.'

'Sure thing.' Roper disappeared into the shadows to return moments later astride his mount, which had been hitched nearby.

They rode out and Roper set a fast pace through the night. Hart was tired but his alertness did not flag. He was accustomed to spending long hours in the saddle and eating whenever he could, and sleep

91

always had to take second place to everything else. He realized that he was retracing his earlier ride, but had needed to ensure that the A Bar M outfit was on its toes.

It was three hours later when Joe Roper broke the silence that had existed between them since leaving A Bar M.

'Circle M is just over yonder,' the cowpuncher said. 'We better make some noise going in or we might draw a slug apiece. These boys are hopping mad about the way their boss was killed. They're raring to go, but with the boss and the ramrod dead, there's no one to give orders.'

Hart saw a light shimmering in the near distance, and could see the deceptive grey light of dawn in the sky to the east. The wind blew free and cold in his face, and his thoughts were sober as they approached the silent ranch. The light turned into a stark square as they drew nearer, and finally showed itself as a window in the ranch house. They were several feet from the big wooden gate enclosing the yard when a low voice called a challenge and they reined in.

'This is Joe Roper and Mike Hart, the Ranger.' Roper glanced at Hart, and they both realized that their vision was increasing by the minute. Day was breaking.

Hart was eager to get to grips with the rustlers. He followed Roper into the yard, where they were checked by a cowboy carrying a rifle.

'Anything happened around here during the night?' Hart asked.

'It's been quiet as Boot Hill. Nothing doing anywhere,' the guard replied.

'Do you have anyone out on the range watching the cattle?' Roper cut in.

'A couple of nighthawks are riding the bounds. We've been expecting trouble from rustlers for some time now.'

'From what I heard, that trouble was due to hit last night,' Hart said quietly. 'Who's running things here?'

'Cal Johnson is the oldest hand on the payroll. He's in the big saddle until word comes from A Bar M. With Ben Murdock dead, the spread belongs to Art Murdock. Do you have any orders for us, Joe?'

'Art ain't in any fit state to pass on orders,' Roper replied. 'I guess the only thing you can do is take heed of what the Ranger says. So far, he's the only one getting things right. He's calling the shots right now, and we'd better hit the trail pronto to check out the herd. If it has been run off then we'll need to do some fighting to get it back.'

'Cal is in the house. Go talk to him. He'll be mighty pleased you've showed up. We're all ready to fight. All we need is someone to tell us what to do.'

Hart rode on to the house, and a squat figure emerged from its dark pile as they reined up in front of the porch.

'Hi, Cal,' Roper called.

'Joe. Am I glad to see you! Have you brought any orders from Art?'

'I've done better than that. This is Mike Hart, the

Ranger. He'll tell you what's going on, and show you how to fight rustlers.'

'Come into the house and we'll talk. I guess you can do with some grub and coffee, huh?'

They went into the house and entered the kitchen. Three tough-looking cowpunchers were sitting at the long table, and the smell of cooking was in the air. Hart did not decline the offer of food, and ate hungrily when it was provided. Cal Johnson, a short fleshy man in his early fifties, asked questions about the future of the Circle M, and Roper explained that while Art Murdock's health was in doubt no one could say with any certainty what would happen.

Hart explained some of the incidents that had involved him, and when he mentioned the outlaws there was a sudden increase in the tension pervading the big room. He went on to mention the rustling, and the 'punchers got to their feet immediately.

'We'll saddle and ride,' one of them said. 'No lowdown, sneaking rustlers are gonna move steers off our range without a fight. All the crew have been champing at the bit, waiting for the word to go.'

'Tell the outfit to saddle up, and be ready to ride when I give the order,' Johnson said. 'I don't want anyone sloping off to fight his own personal war.'

The cowboys departed, and Johnson got to his feet. He was barely six inches above five feet, and drew himself up to his full height as he hitched up his gunbelt.

'I'd better go chase them out of the bunkhouse,' he said. 'We'll be ready to ride by the time you are.'

94

Hart finished his coffee and got to his feet. He looked at the silent Roper. 'You'll be heading back to A Bar M, huh?' he asked.

'I'd better, although I'd rather ride with you. We've had trouble with rustlers for some months, and I'd sure like to get in on the shooting. It's about time the range was cleaned up, and I sure hope you'll take on the farmers after you've settled the rustlers.'

'Not all the farmers are involved,' Hart mused. 'Gedge has got some hardcases around him and they're to blame for the trouble. I got it doped out that Gedge is working for Crane, who brought in the outlaws. Crane has got a lot of questions to answer when I catch up with him.'

Daylight had arrived by the time Hart stepped out to the porch and looked around. Heavy clouds were strung out across the sky, chivvied by the raging wind, and there was a dank feeling in the atmosphere that warned of impending snow. Hart swung into his saddle and looked around. Eight 'punchers were saddling up at the corral, and he grunted with satisfaction as he waited for them. Roper mounted and turned away to ride back to A Bar M.

'Good luck,' he called over his shoulder, as he rode out of the yard.

Hart mounted and went across to a water trough. He let the horse drink, then went on to the corral.

'I could do with a fresh horse,' he said to Johnson.

'Sure thing.' Johnson selected a rangy bay and Hart transferred his gear to it.

The bay tried to throw him when he mounted, but

Hart brought it under control and rode in beside Johnson as the party set out. They headed north, into the wind, and Hart pulled his neckerchief up over his mouth and nose. Johnson set the pace and they cantered towards the Coulee Hills. The range was broken here, with many gullies and ravines, and, when they finally topped a ridge, Johnson halted and uttered an imprecation.

Hart looked over the vista before them; a fairly level area that was devoid of all animal life.

'There was more than a thousand head here last night,' Johnson said bitterly, 'and those thieving sidewinders have taken the lot.'

'They won't be far ahead,' Hart replied grimly. 'Just a few miles. Let's get at it. First we find the direction they took, and then we catch up with them. After that the shooting will start, I reckon.'

They rode on and soon found the tracks of the missing herd. Hart did not need to use his expertise in tracking for the trail left by a thousand head of cattle was clearly sign-posted. They raised their pace to a gallop, and an hour passed before Johnson cautioned them. They halted, and Hart went on ahead with Johnson to a rise in the ground.

They sneaked up to the skyline, and there before them was the Circle M herd, strung out and plodding steadily across the range. Hart counted ten rustlers around the herd, and his pulses quickened at the thought of impending action. He studied the ground, working out their best approach.

'Looks like they're making for Spanish Pass,'

Johnson observed. 'I reckon we could do worse than circle and reach the pass before they arrive. When they show up we'll be able to take them easy.'

'You know the range,' Hart observed. 'Go ahead and do what you think is right. I'll be on hand to join in the fight, but it's your show.'

They went back to their horses and Johnson led the way off to the left. They by-passed the herd and pushed on, keeping under cover, until the trail the cattle were following narrowed to pass through rising ground. Hart looked around with interest.

'I'll leave three men this end,' Johnson said. 'The rest of us will ride through the pass and block the far end. We'll pin the herd in the pass and then pick off the rustlers between us. Any turning back can be stopped by the men at this end.'

'Sounds like a good idea,' Hart said. 'We've got about two hours before the herd shows up, huh?'

'That's what I figure,' Johnson replied.

'I'll stay at the near end,' Hart mused. 'I need to challenge the rustlers before we start shooting – let them know there's a Ranger here.'

'That won't make any difference to them,' Johnson observed. 'You show yourself and they'll shoot you like they would any other man.'

'I'm sure they will.' Hart nodded. 'And when they fire at me I can shoot back.'

Johnson grinned and they returned to the waiting 'punchers. Johnson explained his plan and they agreed whole-heartedly. Three men were detailed to cover the near entrance, and Hart remained with them when Johnson led the others into the pass. Hart looked around for a spot where they could leave their horses safely, and they found a thicket outside the pass. He took his field-glasses from a saddle-bag and looped them around his neck. They checked their guns and then climbed the rock wall of the pass to get to the top.

'The herd will soon be here,' Hart said, spotting dust in the distance.

They settled down to wait, hunching behind rocks to shelter from the flaying wind.

Hart positioned himself where he could watch the approach of the herd. His thoughts rambled in the back of his mind. As soon as possible he wanted to confront Pat Gedge, and then find Bart Crane. After that, he would hunt down Trace Bascombe and his bunch. That was his case simplified, but he was aware that many more ramifications awaited his attention as he hunched his shoulders and steeled himself for the efforts that would have to be summoned up as he progressed through the case.

An hour passed and he began to discern the individual shapes of the approaching cattle. Dust was rising, and only a dozen steers were visible in the van of the herd. The remainder were hidden by the swirling dust. He checked his rifle and pistol again, and satisfied himself that he was ready.

'Say, Hart, there's a rider leaving the herd and riding off to the east,' one of the cowboys said, pointing out the departing rider's position.

Hart lifted his glasses to his eyes, quickly focused

them, and brought Pat Gedge's face into prominence.

'It's Gedge,' he said, 'and he's shown himself at exactly the wrong moment.'

'You could get to your horse and take out after him if you go now,' the cowboy said. 'We can handle this end of the deal.'

Hart shook his head instantly, being well aware of his priorities.

'I'll see this through,' he decided. 'I can always trail Gedge to where he's going. I'll pick him up later.'

They settled down to wait with the wind gusting and moaning around their high, exposed position, and Hart, feeling that the cattle were a long time coming, had to fight against growing impatience.

SEVEN

The leading steers balked at the narrow entrance to the pass and the two rustlers riding point converged on them, swinging ropes and yelling. They induced the leaders to enter the pass, and then the flowing stream of beef on the hoof surged forward to follow blindly. The rustlers entered with the herd, completely surrounded by bellowing, thrusting steers as they continued. Dust rose from the pass, almost obscuring the scene. Hart sat back and waited. The passage of the steers seemed interminable.

Two rustlers brought up the rear, chasing stragglers relentlessly and, as soon as the flow of beef ended, Hart and the three cowpunchers descended to the ground. They had barely picked out positions at the mouth of the pass when the crackling of heavy shooting rang out from the far end.

The shooting was sustained for many minutes, and when the echoes faded, a deathly silence ensued. Presently the ground began to tremor, and dust rose as the herd stampeded back the way it had come.

'We'd better get out of here,' Hart shouted, and

the three 'punchers moved quickly.

They hurried out of the entrance and sought cover in rocks on either side. Minutes later the two riders who had been riding drag appeared at a dead run in a desperate attempt to get clear of the pass before the cattle could overtake them. Hart lifted his rifle but the three cowpunchers opened fire with pistols and the riders were smashed out of their saddles as if by a giant hand. They fell in the path of the advancing herd while their horses galloped away furiously.

The cattle began streaming out of the pass, running blindly back the way they had come, trampling the motionless bodies of the two fallen rustlers. The thunder of pounding hoofs was deafening. Dust flew. Hart moved back slightly, wanting to get a clear view of any other rustlers that might appear. The flow of cattle seemed never-ending, and interminable minutes passed before it began to lessen. Finally the last of the fear-maddened beasts emerged from the pass and blindly followed the main stream.

Hart had not seen any of the other rustlers returning with the herd, and his thoughts were grim as he waited for Johnson and the crew to appear. Minutes later, they came galloping through the dust, and Johnson rode aside and skidded to a halt beside Hart, waving his men on after the herd.

'We got 'em cold,' Johnson said. 'The rustlers never stood a chance. There were eight of them and we knocked five clean out of their saddles. The other three were trampled by the herd when it stampeded.'

His alert gaze spotted the two motionless figures lying in the dust. 'So you got the two riding drag. That means we took care of all of them. I'd better get after the crew. They'll push the herd back to home range when the stampede is over.'

'I've got a job to do now,' Hart replied. 'Pat Gedge rode away from the herd just before it entered the pass, and I need to talk to him.'

'I hope you get him,' Johnson said. 'See you around, huh?'

'Sure thing.' Hart lifted a hand in farewell as Johnson sent his horse on, and moments later he was alone in the dust that hung in the air like a banner. Silence returned slowly. The cold wind began to disperse the dust. Hart went for his horse, his thoughts remote. He had his own business to handle.

He rode to the spot where he had seen Gedge leaving the herd, and soon located the farmer's tracks. He stepped down and studied them before remounting and following them. His preliminary work was at an end. He knew most of the bad men now, and all he had to do was confront them. He glanced at the lowering sky as he rode, trying to gauge when the first snow would come.

Gedge seemed to be in a hurry to get somewhere, judging by the trail his horse was leaving. The prints were deep and far apart, which indicated speed, and Hart pushed his mount to cover the ground. He could feel pangs of hunger gnawing inside him, and was surprised, when he glanced around, to notice that the day had almost passed. He quickened the pace still more, impatient to get to grips with his adversaries.

Gedge was apparently returning to the farming area, for the Coulee Hills were rising up on the skyline. Approaching a farm, Hart saw that Gedge's mount had entered the yard, and he reined into cover and used his field-glasses to check out the area. When he failed to spot Gedge or his horse he went on, riding boldly into the farmyard.

A middle-aged woman came to the door of the small cabin at the far end of the yard and Hart rode towards her. There was a barn on his left, its big door opened wide, and a man holding a shotgun stepped into the aperture. Hart turned aside from the cabin and rode to the barn. The farmer, tall and broad-shouldered, his fleshy face more than half covered by a straggly black beard, levelled the shotgun as Hart reined in.

'You don't need that gun,' Hart said. 'I'm a Texas Ranger on the track of Trace Bascombe and his gang of bank robbers.'

'Do you think they rode in here?' The farmer did not lower his gun. His eyes were filled with suspicion. 'Anyone could ride in here claiming to be a Ranger.'

Hart pulled open his jacket to reveal his law badge. The farmer lowered his shotgun, hesitated, and then stood it against the wall of the barn.

'A man has to be careful these days,' he said. 'I ain't seen anyone looking like a bank robber. I've heard of Bascombe but I ain't ever seen him.'

'I've never seen one who looked the part,' Hart

agreed. 'Have you had any visitors today?'

'Nary a one. We don't get many folks riding in. The farmers are too busy getting prepared for the winter to have time to waste on visiting.'

Hart could see Gedge's tracks in the dust of the yard and wondered why the farmer was lying.

'Pat Gedge is riding around,' he persisted.

'Gedge? Yeah . . . he rode in about thirty minutes ago. I don't look upon him as a visitor. He came to tell me there's a big meeting of farmers at Doolin's farm on Saturday night, and then he rode right out. Said he was in a hurry.'

'I need to speak to Gedge. Where was he heading when he left here?'

'He didn't say, but it looked like he was making for Bill Baga's farm. He said he was gonna call on everyone in the hills.'

Hart was looking over the ground, and saw the prints of Gedge's horse entering the barn. He removed his right glove and eased his right foot out of his stirrup.

'Was there something wrong with Gedge's horse?' he demanded.

'His horse?' The farmer looked surprised. 'What's to do with his horse?'

'It went into your barn and didn't come out again. Is it still in there, with Gedge?'

The farmer firmed his lips and did not reply.

'It's very serious to lie to a Ranger.' Hart was alert as he spoke, and saw a shadow of movement just inside the doorway of the barn, which was gloomy.

He lunged sideways out of his saddle and hit the ground on his left shoulder as he drew his pistol.

A gun crashed inside the barn and a bullet kicked dust into Hart's face before whining away across the yard. Hart fired at the gun flash, his shot narrowly missing the farmer standing in the doorway. He lunged to his feet and ran forward into the barn. The farmer turned and reached for his shotgun, and Hart, in passing, struck him across the back of the head with his pistol.

The farmer went down. Hart entered the barn and hurled himself to the left, his gun lifting to cover the interior of the building. He saw Gedge's horse standing to one side. Gedge was on the ground on hands and knees, his head hanging. Blood was showing on his face and his pistol lay just out of his reach.

Hart went forward and kicked Gedge's gun clear. He grasped the farmer by the scruff of the neck and hauled him to his feet. Gedge was dazed. Hart's bullet had put a bloody groove on his right temple before clipping the top of his ear.

'This is the first real chance I've had to face you since you left the JB ranch,' Hart said. 'If I'd taken you in then I would have saved myself a lot of trouble. I hope the talk we're gonna have will clear up some questions that have been bothering me.'

'I got nothing to say to you,' Gedge replied.

'Why did you attempt to shoot me?'

'I didn't. I was checking my gun and it went off accidentally.'

'So that's the way you want it, huh?' Hart smiled.

105

'OK, we'll do it the hard way, only it won't be hard for me. Get on your horse. I'm on my way to Ashville, and when we get there I'm gonna put you in a cell.'

'You got no reason to arrest me.' Gedge was prepared to brazen it out, but Hart's face showed that he was in no mood to compromise.

'You'd have to prove that before I'd let you go.' Hart grinned. He could see that the farmer in the doorway was beginning to stir. 'Lead your horse outside and don't try to get smart. You've got a lot of talking to do.'

Gedge staggered to his horse and grasped the reins. Hart backed out of the barn as Gedge emerged, covering the farmer with his pistol. He went to his horse and opened a saddle-bag, produced handcuffs, and snapped them on Gedge's wrists. The farmer protested but Hart ignored him. He tied Gedge's reins to his saddle horn, mounted his own horse, and they were riding out of the yard as the farmer in the doorway of the barn was getting to his feet.

'I heard Trace Bascombe talking last night,' Hart said, as he headed in the direction of Ashville. 'He mentioned you by name, and connected you with Bart Crane. I've heard that you're no farmer, so obviously you've been put into the farming community to stir up trouble. You'll make my job a lot easier by telling me about the set-up. How did Crane get Bascombe to throw in with him?'

'I don't know what you're talking about.' Gedge shook his hands, making the handcuffs rattle.

106

'You've made a big mistake arresting me.'

'Ben Murdock was murdered. Someone is gonna hang for that, and right now it looks like you've been elected. If you know anything at all about the killing then you'd be wise to speak up now, because no one else will come forward and tell the truth.'

'Ben Murdock dead? Hell, I didn't even know that. Where was he killed? I've never been within miles of Circle M.'

'What were you doing with the rustlers running off the Circle M herd?'

'I saw them from a distance and rode away fast. I know nothing about rustling, and I wouldn't want to get mixed up in anything to do with cattle ranching.'

'I saw you from a distance as you were leaving the herd. That's good enough for me. I got you dead to rights, Gedge, and you won't wriggle off the hook. If you are telling the truth then you've got to prove it to me. I couldn't settle for anything less even if I wanted to.'

'How can I prove anything?' Gedge complained.

'Where is Bart Crane? He wasn't in Ashville when I was there. When was the last time you saw him, and what did you talk about?'

'I got nothing in common with Crane. He ain't the kind of man I would cross the street to talk to.'

'So if you're not working with Crane then who is paying you to handle your side of the crooked deal? Why were you at the JB ranch, worrying the life out of Mrs Baines? And don't give me that guff about wanting to buy the spread. If you did buy it, it wouldn't be to turn it over to farming. So what gives?'

Gedge shook his head, and Hart knew by the set of the man's features that he would get no information from him.

'Let's push on,' Hart decided. 'Maybe you'll feel easier about talking when I've got you behind bars. There's nothing to beat that hemmed-in feeling to change a man's mind about coming clean, especially when there's a murder charge waiting to be slapped on someone.'

'You won't prove anything against me, not in a hundred years,' Gedge replied.

Hart looked around, realizing that night would fall before he got far. He saw a farm in the distance, and eased to the left to avoid it, aware that every farmer in the Hills could be sympathetic to Gedge. The wind was blowing against the back of his neck, and he decided to make camp for the night, aware that he was still many miles from his objective.

Accustomed as he was to roughing it on the trail, Hart was uncomfortable through the long night. He chose a sheltered spot and made camp, and Gedge was unable to give him any trouble when they settled down. He tied Gedge's ankles together, covered the farmer over with a blanket and, after advising Gedge to sleep, he settled himself in a sitting position with his back to a rock and hunkered down in his slicker to doze away the long hours of darkness. He ignored the discomfort, being inured to the rough life he was forced to lead.

Dawn was coming into the sky when Hart shed his

blanket and stood up to stretch. He checked Gedge and found the farmer as he had left him the night before. Gedge looked as if he had not closed his eyes, and Hart grinned as he prepared a frugal breakfast and shared it with his prisoner. After drinking coffee, he broke camp and they continued to town.

The day was dull and cold, with the eternal wind blowing furiously from behind. Several times Hart saw a flake or two of snow whirling by, and a sense of desperation tried to seep into his mind as he reviewed the situation while continuing. But nothing could shake his confidence that he would overcome the bad men. When he sighted Ashville he reined up, and Gedge, slumped in his saddle, seemed to be more depressed than before.

'Not looking forward to a spell behind bars, huh?' Hart commented.

'You won't be holding me long.' Gedge scowled. 'You're wasting your time, Ranger.'

It was around noon when they hit the main street of the town, and Hart reined in before a small adobe building that had a board nailed above the doorway bearing the word JAIL. He dismounted and trailed his reins as he looked around the quiet street. The bank was next door, seemingly deserted. There was no one out in the cold wind, and Hart stretched to get the kinks out of his tall figure as he tried the door of the jail and found it locked.

'There ain't no law in this town,' Gedge volunteered, cracking his sour expression with a leering grin. 'I told you it would be useless.'

'You're wrong,' Hart replied. 'I'm the law, and I'm here to stay until I finish the job I was sent to do.'

'Crane is the sheriff these days, so why don't you look him up?'

'I'll get round to Crane in due course, and I'm looking forward to that event.'

Hart looked around the street again. He saw a man in a white apron standing in the doorway of the store almost opposite, and beckoned, but the man turned abruptly and disappeared into the store. Gedge laughed.

'No one around here has got the guts to stand up against Crane,' he opined. 'You're on your own against a dozen gun hands who work for Crane, and that ain't the end of it.'

'I killed three of Crane's gun hands when I was last in town,' Hart observed mildly. 'I didn't find them so tough.'

Gedge fell silent, his face sobering. Hart grasped the farmer's arm and dragged him from his saddle. Gedge almost fell when his cramped legs gave way, and Hart hauled him upright. He produced the key to Gedge's handcuffs, unlocked one cuff, then passed the loose cuff under the hitch rail and snapped it back around Gedge's wrist.

'That should hold you until I come back,' Hart said.

'You ain't gonna leave me out here, are you?' Gedge protested.

'You got a better idea?' Hart moved away, his keen gaze searching the street. He went to the bank and entered. The place was deserted, but the sound of his boots on the bare boards brought a man through a doorway in the back wall. 'Howdy,' Hart said. 'I want to get into the jail. Have you any idea where I might pick up the keys?'

'Why would you want to get into the jail?' Surprise laced the man's tone. He was tall and thin, with a worried expression on his wrinkled features that seemed permanent. He was dressed in a dark-blue store suit that was badly creased, giving the impression of a good man running to seed.

'I've got a prisoner I need to put behind bars. I'm Mike Hart, Texas Ranger. I arrested Pat Gedge this morning.'

'You've arrested Gedge?' Astonishment chased worry out of the man's features and his eyes widened. 'Say, you killed Kenyon in the saloon the other night, and a couple more of Crane's gunnies. So you picked up Gedge. And you hope to keep him in jail? I wish you luck, Ranger, but the minute Gedge's friends hear about his bad luck they'll be howling around town like a pack of wolves. I'm Henry Davis, the banker, and I ain't got any respect for the law after the bank was robbed six months ago. The minute the sheriff tried to do something about it he was killed, and Crane took over the law, which meant we didn't get any more law dealing.'

'I've taken over the law now, until the town gets back to normal.'

'Does Crane know that?' Davis shook his head.

'Is he back in town?' Hart countered. 'If he is I'll

see him and lay down the law to him.'

'That I'd like to see. You're up against it, Ranger, and the sooner you realize that, the more chance you'll have of getting out of here alive.'

'Thanks for the advice. Do you reckon the jail keys are in Crane's saloon?'

'I reckon he locked up and threw away the keys when he took over the law,' Davis said, shaking his head.

Hart departed, thin-lipped, but he could not wonder at the banker's negative attitude. He glanced at the motionless Gedge, saw a townsman talking to the farmer, and went back to the jail. The townsman started to move away but paused when Hart called to him.

'Is there a carpenter in the town?' Hart asked.

'Sure. Ben Miller. What do you want him for? Lost the keys to Gedge's handcuffs?'

'No. I'll need him to repair the door of the jail.' Hart moved to the door, thrust forward his left shoulder, and lunged against the woodwork. At the second attempt the door flew inwards with a splintering crash, and Hart turned to the open-mouthed townsman. 'Go tell Miller I need his help,' he said.

The man departed at a run as Hart entered the jail. The big room was dusty, and gave an impression that it had not been opened in months. There was a desk against the back wall, its top littered with discarded papers and files. The door of the big prisoner cage on the left was wide open. The pot-bellied stove in the centre of the room looked defunct, and

Hart shook his head as he turned to the street.

He took Gedge into the jail and clicked the left-hand cuff around a bar in the cage door. When Gedge protested, Hart pushed a chair within the man's reach and Gedge sat down. Hart sat on the chair behind the desk and opened some drawers, grunting in satisfaction when he found a bunch of keys. He went to the cell door, found a key which fitted the big lock, and then removed the cuffs from Gedge and locked him in the cell.

'Now we're in business,' he remarked, and turned to the street door when a man came into the office.

'I'm Ben Miller, the carpenter,' the newcomer declared. 'What's going on?'

'I want you to fix the door.' Hart crossed to the street door and tried without success to find a key on the bunch he had found that fitted the lock. 'You'll need to put a new lock in,' he added.

'Does Bart Crane know about this?' Miller asked. 'I ain't about to start a job if Crane ain't likely to pay for it.'

'Crane doesn't know, but he will soon as I can find him. Can you do the job or not?'

'Sure I can do it. What I want to know for certain is will I get paid for doing it?'

'Will you take the word of a Texas Ranger?'

'I'd rather have Crane giving the order. He's the law around here.'

'Not any more, he ain't. I'm running things now.'

'OK. I'll take your word for it. I'll fetch my tools.'

Hart returned to the desk and straightened up

some of the papers. Dust was covering everything. He opened a door in the back wall and found himself looking into a small room that was fitted out as a bedroom. There was another door in it leading to the back lots, with a key showing in the lock. He opened the door and gazed around outside, then closed and locked it again.

Gedge called to him when he went back into the office. 'Are you gonna light a fire in here?' he demanded. 'It's freezing. And what about some hot food? I ain't eaten in twenty-four hours.'

'Sure, when I get organized,' Hart replied. 'I'm going along to Crane's saloon now, to check if he's showed up.'

'You'd better drop in at the eating-house and ask them to send some food over before you do that in case Crane kills you,' Gedge replied. 'And tell someone out there that I'm in the cage, for the same reason. I want out of here as soon as possible. You won't hold me long.'

Hart went out to the street and saw Miller returning. The carpenter was carrying a tool bag.

'I'll be back shortly,' Hart said. 'Give me a key to the new lock you're going to fit, and lock up here if I ain't back by the time you get through. I'll see you later to square up with you.'

Miller opened a cardboard box and checked the lock inside. He handed one of the two keys to Hart, who put it in his coat pocket.

'You better know that I saw Bart Crane riding into town when I came out of my workshop,' Miller said,

114

as Hart departed. 'He came out of an alley on to the back lots, so it looks like he's been told you're causing trouble in the town. He'll be expecting you, Ranger, so if you know any prayers you better say them before you go into the saloon.'

'I'm on my way there now,' Hart replied. 'I was hoping Crane was back. So long. Do a good job on that door.'

He set off along the sidewalk, making for the saloon, and his keen gaze did not miss the faces peering out of windows he passed by. There was an air of showdown in Ashville, and Hart was certain that it would not be the only one he'd face before he settled this crooked business to his satisfaction.

EIGHT

Hart opened his long coat as he reached the batwings of the saloon, and dropped his right hand down to his side. He could feel the butt of his holstered pistol pressing against the inside of his wrist as he shouldered through the swing doors and looked around. There were just two men in the bar, and one of them was Jenner, the bartender, who was checking bottles on the back of the bar. The other man looked like a gun hand. Jenner swung round when he heard the batwings creak, and his features tensed when he recognized Hart.

'I didn't think I'd see you again,' he called. 'I thought you'd be well on your way back to San Antonio by now.'

'Cut the guff,' Hart replied. 'Where's Crane?'

'Heck, he ain't back from his trip yet, and I don't know when to expect him.'

Hart walked along the bar and passed Jenner as if the man was not there. He continued to the door in the back wall that led into Crane's private quarters.

'Hey, where you going?' Jenner called hastily. 'You

can't go through there.'

'Are you gonna stop me?' Hart swung round to find the twin barrels of a shotgun covering him. Jenner had lifted the weapon from under the bar. 'You must be desperate to pick up a gun against a Ranger,' he observed. 'Put it down before I lose patience with you.'

'Crane would kill me if I let you go through there.' There was a flat tone in Jenner's voice that betrayed tension, and he tightened his grip on the gun. 'I'm only doing my job,' he added.

'You've made your pitch, so put down the gun before I decide you ain't joking. I've opened the jail, so I can take prisoners, but you got no chance to see the inside of it because I don't like men who point guns at me.'

Silence followed. Jenner gulped, his Adam's apple jerking in his throat. Sweat broke out on his forehead as a sigh gusted from him. He wilted slowly, the starch running out of him. The twin muzzles of the shotgun began to waver, and then moved downwards to point at the floor. He half turned and placed the fearsome weapon on the top of the bar before stepping back from it with relief showing on his sweating face.

'You got more sense than I gave you credit for the last time I was in here,' Hart said. 'You're learning fast. Now try for something a little harder. Tell me about Crane, and before you deny he's back I'll tell you that he was seen riding this way a few minutes ago.'

'If he came in the back door then I wouldn't have seen him,' Jenner spoke cautiously.

'So get on with your job and I'll do mine.' Hart continued to the door in the back wall and thrust it open. He entered the living quarters, his hand close to the butt of his holstered gun.

He was in a small room that was unfurnished except for a desk, a safe, a chair and a filing cabinet. A door leading into the rear of the building was ajar, and Hart went to it, his nerves tightening. He found himself in a passage, and stairs at the end on the right gave access to the upper storey. To the left was the back door, and Hart went to it, opened it silently, and peered around the back lots. He saw a small barn about thirty yards behind the saloon, and wondered if that was where Crane stabled his horse.

He closed the door and ascended the stairs. A search of the upper floor revealed nothing. If Crane had returned he was somewhere else, probably getting a report of the incidents that had occurred in town during his absence. He stood motionless in the passage, thinking about the situation. All he wanted right now was to get his hands on Crane.

A door slammed somewhere below and Hart turned instantly to cover the stairs. He heard creaking as someone put weight upon the stairs, and drew his pistol as he prepared to fight his way out of the building.

A head came into view as a man ascended the stairs, and the newcomer paused in shock at the sight of Hart's big figure standing motionless above him.

'Who in hell are you?' he demanded, his right hand lifting towards his left armpit, but he stopped the movement quickly when he saw the gun in Hart's hand.

'I'm waiting to see you, if you are Bart Crane,' Hart responded.

'Did Jenner let you up here?'

Hart shook his head. 'No. He wasn't able to stop me. Are you Crane?'

'Who else would I be? What do you want?'

'Where have you been since you got back to town?' Hart waggled his gun, the muzzle gaping at Crane. 'I'm Mike Hart, Texas Ranger. I've waited a couple of days to see you. I've heard a lot about you, Crane; all of it was bad.'

Hart knew by Crane's changing expression that the saloon-man had heard about him.

'You got no right to come busting in here as if you owned the place,' Crane said. He was tall, heavily built, his face fleshy and smooth. He was clean-shaven except for a thick moustache, and his dark sideburns reached down below his ears. His long coat was of good quality, and the flat-crowned hat he was wearing seemed to be almost new.

'I've got the right to go where I please in the pursuit of criminals,' Hart said.

'I haven't broken the law. What do you want to see me about?'

'Your association with Trace Bascombe, among other things.'

'Bascombe? Never heard of him.'

'Well, he knows you. I heard him talking about you a couple of nights ago like the two of you were old friends. From what he said, I reckoned you had a big deal cooking. How'd you manage to talk him into quitting his regular line of work? He robbed the bank here in Ashville about six months ago, and since then he's been working hand in glove with you. Come on up here and we'll talk about your business interests. You've also got a bunch of rustlers at work on this range, and Pat Gedge, the farmer, is working for you, rousing up the farming community to cause trouble with the ranchers. You sure got a handful of irons in the fire, Crane.'

Crane gazed into the muzzle of Hart's gun for what seemed an eternity, then heaved a long sigh and mounted the remaining stairs. He half-turned away from Hart when he reached the top stair, and Hart was expecting the saloon-man to reach for the gun in his shoulder holster. But Crane seemed to miss his footing on the last step and grasped the hand rail with his left hand. His right hand lifted slightly, and the next instant a .41 calibre hideout pistol slid down from his wrist on a quick-draw rig and fitted neatly into his hand.

Hart hurled himself sideways to the floor, his pistol blasting out the silence with a single shot. Crane fired at almost the same instant, and Hart felt the smack of a bullet in the outside of his left thigh just below the hip. Crane's face was contorted in desperation. Hart's bullet took him in the right forearm and he spun away, his boots rapping on the bare

120

boards. He came swinging back to face Hart again, reaching for the pistol in his shoulder holster.

Crane's mouth was agape, although no sound issued from it. Sweat was beading his forehead. He drew his pistol speedily, despite the blood streaming from his forearm. Hart squeezed his trigger again. The big weapon hammered and a slug thumped into Crane's right shoulder. Crane fell awkwardly, his gun spilling from his hand.

Hart got to his feet. His ears were protesting at the noise of the shots, and the smell of burned powder was thick in his nostrils. He holstered his gun and picked up the weapon Crane had dropped. Pain was spreading through his left thigh and he could feel blood seeping down the limb. He examined Crane. The saloon-man was unconscious. His right shoulder had been dusted both sides and blood was leaking fast. Hart's first shot had struck the quick-fire rig on Crane's right forearm and it had been half-torn from the limb.

Footsteps sounded on the stairs. Hart turned quickly, pressing his left hand against the wound in his upper thigh. Pain was knifing through the hip and travelling down to his left knee. He clenched his teeth and peered down the stairs, gun ready.

Jenner was ascending the stairs, holding his shotgun, and lifted the weapon when he saw Hart looking down at him.

'Drop it,' Hart rapped.

Jenner paused for a split second, and then brought the gun up into the aim. Hart fired instantly, not prepared to take any chances against a scatter-gun. Jenner took the slug between his eyes and pitched over backwards down the stairs. The shotgun exploded raucously and a whirling load of buckshot blasted upwards through the ceiling.

Hart watched Jenner's body crumple at the foot of the stairs. A trickle of blood was dribbling from the neat round hole in Jenner's forehead. Hart's ears were protesting at the noise of the shooting and he yawned to ease them. He started down the stairs, pistol ready, and reached the bar without incident. The man who had been in the saloon at Hart's entrance was still at the bar, drinking, showing no indication of having heard the shooting.

'There's a doctor in town, huh?' Hart demanded.

'Yeah. Name of Chilvers.'

'Go fetch him. Tell him Crane is bad hurt.'

The man turned away from the bar and walked steadily to the batwings. Hart went behind the bar and helped himself to a drink. He reloaded his pistol and then took another drink. A few moments later, a tall, dark-haired man entered the saloon. He was carrying a medical bag, and paused when he saw Hart.

'Where's Crane?' he demanded curtly.

'Top of the stairs.' Hart followed the doctor, favouring his left leg, and they stepped over Jenner's body to ascend the stairs. The doctor tut-tutted at the sight of the bartender. Hart could tell that his own wound was superficial, and his concern was that Crane would survive to talk about his crooked career.

'I'll need some help to get him over to my office.'
Chilvers spoke with the imperturbability of a man
who had seen everything during his long medical
career. 'You're showing blood. Want me to take a
look at it?'

'Later. What you can do is tell me if Crane has any
men around town who might want to toss lead at
me.'

'If there are they'll come up on you from behind.'
Chilvers laughed harshly. 'Crane was no slouch with
a gun, and it looks like he tried his fast-draw on you
but it didn't work. You killed Kenyon from an even
break the other day, huh?'

'And I've got some more killing to do before this
bad business is settled.' Hart watched the doctor
working at staunching the blood running from
Crane's wounds. 'How did you leave Art Murdock?
You were tending him when I called at A Bar M.'

'Art will live. He's tough as whang leather. They'd
have to beat him to death with a big stick to finish
him off. You got any help in your job or are you working alone?'

'I never needed any gun help before, and they
wouldn't send anyone even if I asked. We have to get
by the best way we can. I've opened up the jail, so
you'll find me there if you want me. If Crane's fit to
be moved after you've treated him then have him
brought to the jail. He'll be under arrest a long
time.'

'You'll need some help.' Chilvers straightened.
'Walt Halfnight used to be the town jailer until Crane

took over the law, and I saw him this morning, as a matter of fact. He's working with Bill Taylor, the undertaker, and the way he was talking, I'd say he isn't keen on the job. If you offer him his old job at the jail he'd jump at it.'

'Where will I find him?' Hart asked.

'Taylor's mortuary is on the back lots behind Dan Harper's store. You can get to it along any alley.'

'Thanks.' Hart turned away. 'I'll check with you later about Crane's condition.'

He departed quickly, limping as pain spread through his thigh, and was surprised, on reaching the street, to find that no sightseers were around. He walked to the store and turned into the alley beside it. When he emerged on the back lots he saw a large building some fifty yards across the lots, and there were two men standing in the gateway of a large yard, in which stood a black, glass-panelled hearse. They watched Hart's approach, and he touched a finger to his hat when he confronted them.

'Howdy. I'm looking for Walt Halfnight,' Hart said. 'I'm Mike Hart, Texas Ranger. I've just opened up the town jail and I need a jailer. I heard that Halfnight used to fill that job.'

'I'm Halfnight.' The shorter of the two men grinned. 'I'm sure glad to see you! We heard some shooting a while back, and I told Bill there'd be more customers to handle. But I'm ready to go back to my old job. I never liked working here, and Bill knows that. When do you want me to start? I can walk into that jail right now and take over like I've never been away.'

'I need you now. I got Pat Gedge behind bars, and I sure expect a rush of custom when word gets around that I'm cleaning up. Jenner is lying dead in Crane's saloon, and Crane is lucky to be in the Doc's hands instead of waiting for you to deal with him.'

'I better get over to the saloon right away.' Taylor grinned at the prospect of business and clapped a hand on Halfnight's shoulder. 'Good luck, Walt. There'll be a job here for you if this doesn't work out.'

'Thanks, Bill.'

Taylor hurried away, and Hart walked back to the street with Halfnight accompanying him. They reached the jail to find two riders standing there, watching Miller, the carpenter, at work, their mounts waiting with trailing reins. Hart was surprised when he recognized Charlene Murdock and Joe Roper. The girl looked worried. Her face was pale and showing strain. Her eyes were narrowed, filled with stress, but she smiled when she saw Hart.

'So you've started cleaning up the town,' she observed. 'What was the shooting about?'

Hart told them as he led the way into the law office. Joe Roper grinned.

'I sure wish I could have seen you in action,' he said. 'We came to tell you there's a chance of catching the rest of those rustlers who've been hitting us. We've seen signs of activity on our south range so we ran a herd out there as bait, and it looks like the rustlers are gonna strike. They're moving around in that area. Do you wanta get in on the kill?'

'We need you along,' Charlene said.

'Sure.' Hart nodded. 'I also want to come up with Trace Bascombe and the rest of his bunch. There's nothing more I can do around here at the moment. Crane is out of it, but I am a little concerned that his men will show up and try and take over again. I heard that Crane has two cattle ranches in the county. We'll go for the rustlers, and then take in Crane's spreads to check on his crews. I want all loose ends tied up before it snows, and it sure feels like I don't have much time left.'

'We shall have enough men to take care of all that,' Charlene said. 'Can you ride with us now?'

Hart nodded and turned to Halfnight. 'Walt, all you've got to do is keep Gedge in here, and handle Crane if the doc says he's well enough to stay behind bars. What we need is a deputy to take charge. Did the sheriff have any helpers when he was in office?'

'They were dismissed by Crane after the sheriff was killed,' Halfnight said. 'That's when I lost my job, and things have been pretty bad around here since.'

'We got one of the ex-deputies working on our spread,' Roper said. 'Cal Piercey. He's getting long in the tooth but he's a good worker, and he tried his best when he was wearing a law star. Why don't you ask him to take over here now Crane is out of it? From how Piercey talks, I'd say he'd come back pronto.'

Hart went to the desk and jerked open a drawer. He found a deputy badge and slipped it into a pocket.

126

'Good luck.' Halfnight crossed to a gun rack in a corner, selected a shotgun, and sat down behind the desk to clean it.

Hart led the way out to the street. He was well satisfied with the way the situation was turning. His gaze instinctively searched his surroundings as he paused, and he stiffened when he saw a man appearing in an alley across the street. The man's right hand made a sudden movement towards a holstered gun, and Hart flowed into action.

Hart made a fast draw as Joe Roper came up on his right, and his elbow thudded against Roper's chest, the impact sending his pistol flying from his hand. The cowboy gasped as Hart spun him around and snatched the pistol from his holster. A mere split second had passed, but it was sufficient to give the man across the street an edge that the speed of his draw could not have done. A shot blasted, and Hart felt the tug of a bullet as it passed through the crown of his hat. He dropped to one knee, Roper's gun in his left hand, and returned fire instantly.

The crash of the shooting threw harsh echoes across the town. Hart narrowed his eyes, viewing the unknown man through a haze of gunsmoke. His shot had struck the man in the centre of the chest, sending him backwards against the corner of the building opposite, and echoes faded slowly as he collapsed into the dust.

Roper picked up Hart's gun and returned it to him, shaking his head in admiration. 'That was some shooting,' he said. 'And I should have known better than to come up on your right. He might have killed you.'

Hart removed his Stetson and stuck a finger through the bullet hole. 'He wasn't far off the target,' he replied. 'Let's go take a look at him.'

They crossed the street and Roper bent over the man, who was lying on his face. He turned the body over and straightened.

'It's Deke Harlan,' he said. 'You killed his three pards the other night. Kenyon was one of them.'

'There was one who got away that night.' Hart nodded. 'So now we better ride. Once I clean up the range the rest should be easy.'

They fetched their horses and rode out, hitting a gallop as soon as they reached the open trail. The action seemed interminable, Hart told himself. He seemed to be lurching from one crisis to another. The trail apparently had no ending – but he wouldn't have wanted it any other way. He glanced critically at the lowering sky. The wind had not slackened and the threat of snow was now very real. He shivered to think of trying to trail rustlers through snow drifts, and the thought made him quicken the pace.

It was dark when they reached A Bar M, and a guard challenged them as they approached. Hart could hardly see a hand in front of his face. He heard voices off in the shadows as they continued across the yard to the ranch house. There were no lights anywhere. Hoofs suddenly clattered somewhere in the darkness, horses and riders anonymous in the night, and they came into the ranch yard at a run.

Hart was alarmed. His pistol slid into his hand. Roper called out a challenge, and his voice was drowned out by the blasting roar of several six-guns. Flashes split the darkness and shots hammered raucously. Hart leaned sideways and swiped Charlene out of her saddle as the spiteful crackle of closely passing lead warned that they were the targets of this unexpected attack.

Charlene cried out in shock as she fell from her saddle. She hit the ground hard, was half-stunned, and lay motionless while her horse cavorted nervously, its steel-shod hoofs slamming perilously close to her head. Hart came diving out of leather, and sprawled beside the girl, his pistol flaming as he bought into the action. The next instant he groaned, crumpled, and fell inertly at the girl's side.

NINE

Hart was in the act of swinging out of his saddle when a bullet zipped out of the darkness and creased his skull just above the left ear. He felt no pain as he fell senseless. The shooting faded, and sight and sound disappeared abruptly. He was barely aware of hitting the ground; unconscious as he rolled against the cowering girl.

Charlene was shocked. Fear was vibrant in her mind as she forced herself to her knees and bent over Hart. The shooting had cut off as suddenly as it began, and she heard a number of riders galloping away from the ranch. Joe Roper was on one knee, firing rapidly into the shadows, and he did not desist until Charlene called to him for help.

Roper reloaded his pistol and holstered it before moving to Charlene's side. He blinked rapidly several times to rid his gaze of the dazzle caused by gun flashes, and almost fell over Hart's inert body. He gazed into the girl's pallid face as he reached out and grasped her arm.

'Is he hurt bad?' Roper demanded.

'I can't tell. I can't see anything in this light. Let's get him into the house.'

'Take his feet.' Roper grasped Hart's shoulders, and grunted as he lifted the Ranger's heavy figure.

A rifle opened fire at a great distance from the house, splitting the darkness with orange muzzle flame. Three 44.40 slugs whined through the night. Charlene shivered as she bent to take hold of Hart's legs, and she had to use all of her strength to hold them clear of the ground as they staggered towards the dark pile of the house. A harsh voice called a challenge from the porch, and Charlene replied angrily.

'Who do you think we are?' she retorted. 'Come and help us, Hemp. The Ranger has been hit.'

The ranch foreman came off the porch and took Hart's weight. Charlene ran ahead to open the front door, and Hart was carried inside. The girl moved through the darkness with the sure movements of one completely familiar with the topography of the big room, and unerringly found the long table in its centre. Her deft fingers located a match and she lit the wick of the ornate lamp standing in the centre of the table.

'That will attract shooting,' Benteen said as yellow glare flooded the room.

'I've had enough of this fiddling around in the dark,' Charlene replied angrily. 'Hemp, I want you to put shutters up at the windows and pickets out to keep raiders from coming in close and tossing lead at us. If we haven't got enough men for the job then hire more guns.'

Benteen did not reply. He and Roper eased Hart down on a horsehair couch, and Charlene gasped in shock when she saw a great amount of blood on the left side of Hart's head. Benteen eased off Hart's Stetson and examined the area around the Ranger's ear.

'It ain't so bad,' the big foreman said. 'He's lost some hair, but the wound is only a gouge. It looks like he's got a hard skull.'

'He's coming to,' Roper observed as Hart groaned.

Charlene hurried out to the kitchen for a pan of water and a cloth and, when she returned, Hart was trying to push himself into a sitting position. His taut features were pale and he was holding a hand to his head. Blood had crusted around his ear.

'Did a horse kick me?' Hart demanded.

'Be still and let me look at you,' Charlene reproved.

'It's no more than a scratch,' Hart replied humourlessly. 'What happened?'

Roper explained, and Benteen cut in, 'The place has been shot up several times since noon. I reckon the rustlers are trying to hold us here while they run off the beef.'

'So why didn't you take out after them?' Charlene demanded.

'And leave the ranch defenceless with your pa lying helpless in his bed?' Benteen countered. 'The rustlers would sure have liked that, huh?'

'You did right,' Hart said, suffering Charlene's ministrations.

The girl sponged blood from his ear and face, and Hart took the cloth from her and wiped his forehead.

'That's better,' he said. 'I reckon a cup of coffee would go down well. Then we'd better head out to where you left that herd.'

'It would be better if you waited for morning before moving out,' Charlene suggested. 'If the herd has been stolen you won't be able to do anything until daylight. You'd be better off resting up for a few hours.'

Hart did not argue. His head was aching; the wound above his ear throbbing painfully. He allowed his shoulders to slump as Charlene applied a bandage to his head. The girl went into the kitchen and made coffee, and Hart sighed thankfully as he drank a cup of it. He settled back on the couch, lowered his head gingerly to a cushion, and then closed his eyes. Benteen and Roper departed quietly for the bunkhouse as Charlene turned down the lamp, and Hart slept.

It was barely daylight when Hart opened his eyes. The wind was gusting around the house, tearing at loose boards and rattling windows. He sat up, clutching at his aching head. He looked around with narrowed eyes, wondering where he was until his mind slipped into focus and his memory returned.

The front door was pushed open and Benteen appeared. The foreman halted in mid-stride when Hart's pistol appeared in his hand to cover him. Hart returned the weapon to its holster with a swift movement, apologizing for his reaction. He reached for his Stetson, and grimaced when he saw yet another bullet hole in it.

'It's about time we lit out,' Benteen said. 'Hank Tolliver just rode in from watching the herd from a distance. He's got a bullet in his shoulder, and was lucky to make it back to the spread. He reckoned a dozen rustlers hit the herd in the early hours. They're hazing them beeves to the south-west. I've got the crew ready to ride. We're waiting on you now. Your horse is ready.'

Charlene opened the inner door. She was holding a large plate, and the appetising smell of cooked food informed Hart that he was ravenously hungry.

'How are you feeling this morning?' Charlene enquired.

'I'm fine,' Hart replied. 'We're about to ride out. The herd has been taken.'

'You'll have to eat breakfast before I permit you to leave,' Charlene retorted. 'Sit down.'

'We'll be ready to ride in about ten minutes,' Benteen said tactfully. 'You got time to eat.'

Hart sighed and dropped into a seat at the table, the movement warning that the wound in his left thigh was not yet healed. He became aware that he was not looking forward to action with his usual eagerness for duty, and figured that his reluctance was due to the head wound he had sustained. He ate steadily, and then swallowed a cup of strong coffee, which did much to restore his natural aggression.

'Thanks, Charlene,' he said as he got to his feet. He put a hand to his head as he senses swirled with the sudden movement. 'I hope Benteen has arranged sufficient cover here while we're out after those rustlers.'

'Hemp does his job well, despite the way I rail at him,' Charlene replied. 'I wish I was riding with you.'

'I'm glad you ain't.' Hart grinned and departed to find ten riders sitting their mounts in the yard. Roper and Benteen were standing on the porch, their horses tethered to the rail in front, and Hart's horse was with them, ready-saddled.

They mounted and rode out, and Benteen set a fast pace to the south. Hart looked around. He fancied that Benteen and the crew could handle the rustlers, and he was impatient to check out the farmers before getting after Bascombe and the outlaws. But it was imperative that he took part in the action against the rustlers, and suppressed his impatience and settled down to the job in hand.

Three hours of riding found them heading into a range of hills, and they picked up the tracks of several hundred steers. Benteen looked neither left nor right as he rode, and his fast pace covered the miles that lay between them and the herd. Eventually, someone reported seeing dust ahead, and Hart drew his pistol and checked it as they continued.

Benteen halted the crew and went on ahead to peer over a ridge. He came back with a grin on his rugged face.

'We got them dead to right, boys,' he said. 'I'll take half of you with me and we'll circle and push on ahead to come at them from the front.'

'I'll ride with the rest from here,' Hart said. 'If one or two of the rustlers manage to slip away you can let them go, and I'll trail them. The business might be over for you when you get the herd back, but I've still got a deal of work to do, and I could do with a break.'

'Sure thing.' Benteen picked his men and they rode out to the right in a wide circle to get ahead of the herd.

Hart moved up the ridge and peered over the crest. He saw the tail end of the rustled herd passing over another ridge ahead, and counted seven rustlers before they vanished from sight. He dismounted and sat on a mound, closing his eyes and holding his head in his hands. He could have wished for a delay in these proceedings, but duty was a harsh mistress, and he summoned up reserves of determination.

Joe Roper had remained with the cowboys waiting with Hart, and he approached Hart some twenty minutes after Benteen had ridden away.

'I reckon we better be moving in,' he said. 'We need to be on hand when Benteen strikes from ahead.'

'Sure thing.' Hart returned to his saddle.

They rode on at a fast clip, and, as they breasted

yet another rise, the sound of rapid gunfire came to them, echoing sullenly in the far reaches of the illimitable range. They hit the top of the ridge and saw the herd in the middle distance, already stretching out in a stampede. Gunsmoke was blossoming around the rustlers as they engaged Benteen and his men.

Hart drew his pistol and checked its loads. They pushed forward in a gallop that took them hammering towards the herd. Gunfire blasted rapidly. Two rustlers fell from their saddles, and when Hart and the crew with him opened fire, the rustlers were quick to read the situation. They split to left and right and made a run for it. The cowboys cut loose with everything they had, and Hart shook his head when all the rustlers were knocked out of their saddles.

Benteen appeared, looming up out of the broiling dust like a phantom of the plains. He ordered the 'punchers to go for the herd, and reined in beside Hart.

'That wasn't so bad,' he observed with a grin. 'Only one of them got away. He headed out fast to the west. We let him go. Come on, I'll show you where he lit out.'

They rode on after the herd, moving to the right of the dust that was billowing in the wake of the running cattle. Benteen did not break his stride as he went on after the herd, but pointed to the west, and Hart saw a rider in the distance, galloping away as if a hundred devils were on his back trail.

'I'll come back to the ranch later,' Hart said, and Benteen lifted a hand and spurred away.

Hart took out after the fleeing rustler, his big black raising dust as it hammered in pursuit. The wind was coming at him from his right and he pulled up the collar of his coat. He was not surprised when his quarry suddenly turned to the north and continued, for it was in that direction the farmers lived and the outlaws lurked in lonely places. Hart took note of the appearance of the horse and how the rustler was dressed, and continued.

The rustler must have had a definite destination in mind for he did not slacken speed. Hart trailed him carefully, never getting within seeing distance, and followed as if attached to the fugitive with a lariat. They passed to the west of A Bar M, and Hart wondered what was in the rustler's mind. The Coulee Hills were to the north-west, and they did not appear to get any nearer as two hours passed.

Hart had accepted that the rustler was making for the farming community, but the man suddenly veered to his left and rode west. Hart tested his memory of Captain Buckbee's map back in San Antonio and decided that the rustler was making for the town of Elm Ridge, which lay to the west of the area where he was operating.

Night was almost upon them when Hart finally topped a ridge and saw the wide main street of a small town before him. His quarry was just a dim shadow ahead, and Hart urged the black on in order to keep the man in view. He paused at the start of the street and watched his man ride into the stable. A sign at his elbow proclaimed that he had arrived at Elm Ridge, and he rode slowly along the street towards the livery barn.

He was waiting in the shadows of an alley opposite the stable with his horse standing with trailing reins at his back when his man emerged from the barn and paused under the lantern burning over the doorway. It was poor light, but sufficient to permit Hart's keen eyes to identify the rustler he had been following. The man headed along the street, and Hart watched him enter a saloon.

Hart took his horse across the street and put the animal in a stall. An ostler appeared and Hart thrust a dollar into the man's ready hand.

'Take care of him,' he ordered. 'Give him water and grain him. I'm in a hurry.'

He left immediately and went along the street. Peering into the saloon through a window in an alley, he saw his quarry sitting at a gaming table with two men who were listening intently to what the rustler had to say. Hart frowned as he watched. The two men looked familiar, and he racked his memory for names to fit their faces. The nearer of the two was stocky, fleshy, in his thirties, with a moon-face and bushy black eyebrows that met over narrowed brown eyes. The other was tall and thin, clean-shaven, and had a white scar on the right side of his face which extended from the side of his mouth to the lobe of his ear. He was at least forty-five years old.

Hart caught his breath as he took in details of the older man. The last time he had seen that scarred face, the hard case had been escaping with a girl hostage who had later been found murdered. Trace Bascombe! Hart gazed at the bank robber with glinting eyes. He had been praying that their trails would cross again, and here was Bascombe in a position to be taken. He looked over the fat man with Bascombe and decided that he was Taco Tate, Bascombe's closest sidekick.

It was in Hart to enter the saloon and confront the two outlaws. He needed them, dead or alive, if he were to close his case. But he controlled his impatience. The rustler was talking at great length to Bascombe, and Hart realized that his face, too, was familiar – one he must have seen on a wanted poster in Captain Buckbee's office. He released his pent-up breath in a bitter sigh, aware that now was not the time for a showdown. There were several hardcases near Bascombe who might also be members of the gang. He decided to hold off until he had gained an insight to the situation.

A man passed the mouth of the alley and hurried into the saloon. Hart watched through the window and saw the newcomer pause on the threshold of the big room with the batwings swinging at his back. Hart tensed. It was the ostler from the stable, and the man glanced around the room before hurrying to the table where Bascombe was seated. There followed an animated conversation in which the ostler waved his arms to emphasize his words, and Bascombe got to his feet whilst drawing his pistol.

Hart backed away from the window as the outlaws and the rustler hurried to the door, followed by four other gun-hung hardcases. The next instant they were on the sidewalk, and Bascombe's harsh voice floated easily to Hart's ears.

'You damn greenhorn, Lambert. You've led that Ranger right here into the town. Get the men together and hunt him down. We can't afford to have him poking around now. Taco, fetch the horses. We'll ride out, but I can't go far until Crane has shown up. He's supposed to be here now with the dough he owes us. Come on, get moving. That Ranger is hell on wheels. I want him put out of it before morning. You got that, Lambert? He followed you here so you get rid of him.'

'Better put a man in my barn in case that Ranger comes back for his horse,' said the ostler.

'That's a good idea.' Bascombe nodded. 'You do that now, Lambert, and when you've killed the Ranger you can come on to Ashville. I'm going there to have a showdown with Crane. He's dragging his feet with his side of the deal, and I'm gonna teach him a lesson. We'll put him out of it and grab all that range and cattle for ourselves. Now get to it. Let's hit our saddles and ride.'

Hart remained in the deep shadows of the alley, fighting an impulse to start the showdown immediately. But he reasoned that the odds were too long against him and thrust his pistol deep into its holster. His time would come, he told himself, and sneaked along the sidewalk behind the half dozen outlaws as they headed for the livery barn. At least, he knew where the gang was heading, and he meant to play his cards right and be in the right spot when the showdown finally broke.

TEN

Hart remained in cover until the outlaws had emerged from the stable and cantered out of town at a fast clip. His tension eased when they vanished into the stormy night, and he drew a deep breath and shook his head, hoping it would not be the last time he saw them. He watched the ostler and Lambert, the rustler, standing in the doorway of the barn, chatting like old friends, until the ostler shrugged his shoulders and faded back into the interior of the stable. Lambert followed, and Hart moved forward silently. He needed to make tracks fast, for he wanted to be in Ashville before Bascombe in order to arrange a reception, and needed to visit A Bar M before heading for a showdown with the outlaws.

He slipped into the barn and eased into the shadows. The ostler had disappeared into his office, and Hart saw Lambert saddling his horse. He cat-footed forward, easing his pistol out of his holster as he did so, and paused behind the rustler.

'Aren't you supposed to be looking for me?' Hart demanded.

Lambert swung round quickly, his hand reaching for his pistol, but he froze when he saw Hart, and raised his hands quickly.

'Is this a hold-up?' he demanded.

'It's the end of your activities as a rustler,' Hart replied. 'I'm arresting you.'

'You got the wrong man!'

'Don't try that. It's a waste of time. I followed you all the way from A Bar M range. Your rustling pards had the hell shot out of them, and I trailed you right to the saloon in this town, and saw you reporting to Trace Bascombe.'

'Who's Trace Bascombe?'

'Cut that out. I got you dead to rights. Get rid of your pistol, and do it slow. I'm cleaning up now, and you're one of the lucky ones. A lot of your pards are slated for Boot Hill, and that's where you'll wind up if you give me any trouble. So let's get moving. You'll be behind bars tonight while I'm riding back to Ashville.'

Lambert disarmed himself, his expression showing disgust at having been taken so easily. Hart grasped Lambert's shoulder and pushed him toward the street.

'I saw a law office just this side of the saloon,' he said. 'Make for it, and don't ask for trouble.'

Lambert obeyed reluctantly and they went to the office. Lambert opened the door and entered and Hart followed closely. A deputy sheriff looked up from the mail-order book he was scanning. He was a big man with a fleshy face, and his blue eyes narrowed as he took in Lambert's appearance and his raised hands.

'What is this?' he demanded. 'What gives?'

'I'm Mike Hart, Texas Ranger.' Hart closed the door with a boot heel. 'This guy is Lambert, a rustler. I followed him from the A Bar M herd after the crew attacked a gang of rustlers. He led me here, and met Trace Bascombe, the bank robber, in the saloon.'

A variety of expressions flitted across the deputy's fleshy face as he took in the import of Hart's report.

'Heck, is this some kind of a bluff you're running?' he demanded. 'There ain't no outlaws around here.'

'Not now there ain't. They just pulled out. Put Lambert behind bars and hold him. He's guilty of rustling. I'll come back to you when I've settled the outlaws. I have to head back to Ashville pronto. What's your name, Deputy?'

'Dave Simpson. This is a quiet town. I ain't never had any trouble here.'

'You're still quiet. The outlaws won't be back. Put Lambert away and I'll hit the trail after Bascombe.'

Simpson picked up a bunch of keys and led the way into the cell block at the rear of the office. Hart saw Lambert locked in a cell and then left hurriedly. He ignored further questions from Simpson and went back to the livery barn for his horse. Saddling up, he rode out and headed directly for A Bar M through the uneasy darkness, the wind tearing at him and sending chills striking through his body.

Tiredness and hunger assailed Hart during the long ride. He wondered if Bascombe would camp for the night. He needed to get to Ashville before the outlaws, and kept riding, picking his way across the dark range, relying upon his uncanny sense of direction to keep him on track. The night was interminable as he rode, and he thought it would never pass, but eventually there was a gradual lightening in the sky that heralded the coming day, and when his range of sight increased he looked around for landmarks.

Two miles on, he reached the valley in which A Bar M was situated and rode into it, turning right and heading south. Dawn was breaking when the cluster of ranch buildings came into view, and he sighed with relief as he approached the yard. The ceaseless wind seemed even stronger as daylight strengthened.

Joe Roper, carrying a rifle, appeared from the open doorway of the barn as Hart rode across the yard. Roper recognized Hart and called a greeting. Hart slid out of his saddle and handed his reins to the cowboy.

'Take care of the horse, Joe, and throw my gear on a good remount. I need to get to Ashville soon as possible.'

'Sure thing. We killed all those rustlers and turned the herd back towards the spread. Did you catch that rustler you lit out after?'

Hart gave a sparse account of his actions subsequent to leaving the herd, and Roper uttered an exclamation when he learned about the outlaws.

'You've got them in the palm of your hand,' he said. 'The outfit will wanta ride into town with you

146

when they hear about this. Benteen went across to the house about ten minutes ago. It's a habit of his. Charlene makes him breakfast. I'll have a remount ready for you in ten minutes.'

'Thanks, Joe. I could sure do with some coffee.'

Hart walked across to the house and rapped on the door, which was opened by Charlene herself. The girl gasped at the sight of him and stepped back to admit him. Hart staggered as he entered.

'I was angry when the crew came back and said you'd taken out alone after an escaping rustler,' Charlene said. 'Hemp should have sent a couple of riders to assist you.'

'I'm glad he didn't.' Hart smiled at Benteen, who was sitting at the big table with a breakfast plate before him. 'That coffee smells good,' he observed.

'You shall have some, and I expect breakfast would not come amiss,' the girl observed. 'Sit down at the table.'

Hart joined Benteen, and narrated his experiences after leaving the herd. The foreman swallowed hard when Bascombe was mentioned.

'Do you want the outfit to ride into town with you?' he asked. 'That gang has caused a lot of trouble around here, and we'd like to be in at the death.'

'I was hoping you'd say that. Bascombe isn't aware that Crane is wounded and in custody. It'll be the perfect set-up, if I can be in Ashville waiting for the gang to ride in.'

'I'll get the outfit ready.' Benteen got to his feet and hurried out of the house.

Hart dared not relax. Charlene brought him coffee and he drank it eagerly. When the girl put a filled plate of hot food before him he fell to eating with gusto.

Charlene sat down opposite him, but did not interrupt his meal. Hart finished with another cup of coffee and thanked the girl profusely as he got to his feet. She arose, her face showing concern, as he started for the door.

'Surely you don't have to leave so soon,' she observed. 'You look as if you could sleep for thirty-six hours.'

Hart nodded. 'You've hit the nail on the head,' he admitted, 'but I've reached a crucial time in my business and a delay could cost me dearly.' He explained the situation and Charlene's expression changed when she realized the gravity of what he was doing. 'How is your father?' he asked.

'Making progress, but it's going to be a long job, I'm afraid.' She sighed heavily. 'Will you be able to finish this crookedness, or have the outlaws got too firm a hold to be beaten?'

'They're as good as finished, and the sooner I get started the sooner the end will come about. Stick close by the house, and don't take any chances, huh?'

She nodded, and he departed to find eight riders ready-saddled and awaiting him. Joe Roper had a remount waiting, and Hart stepped up into the saddle. He reined in beside Benteen.

'Have you left enough men here to take care of the place?' he asked.

Benteen nodded. 'Anyone riding in here looking for trouble will find more than he can chew on,' he replied.

They set out at a fast clip, and Hart had to fight against tiredness as they hammered along the trail to town. The wind chivvied at them continually, but it was coming from behind now, and Hart pulled up his collar around his ears. He could hear the wind whistling through one of the bullet holes in the crown of his hat, and made a mental note to buy a new Stetson as soon as he was able.

They topped a rise and reined in quickly. A buggy was coming towards them along the trail, and Hart tensed when he recognized Widow Baines driving the rig. The woman was whipping the horse, and they scattered as the vehicle threatened to run them down. Benteen swung in beside the horse and grasped the reins, bringing the buggy to a halt.

'Why the all-fired hurry, Miz Baines?' Benteen asked.

'I've been run off my ranch,' she replied, pressing her hands to her face and weeping.

Hart stepped down from his saddle and went to her side. She started nervously when he grasped her hand, and looked up at him appealingly.

'Can you help me? Some of Gedge's farmer friends turned up at my place in the night. It was frightening. My three riders and the two cowboys Charlene sent to guard me tried to fight them off and all were shot. Pete O'Hara was staying with me, and they killed him, too. I got away from the ranch, and I'm heading for A Bar M. Charlene told me I could always turn to her if I needed help.'

'Well, you go right ahead to the big ranch,' Benteen said. 'No one is gonna bother you now.' He glanced at Hart. 'I guess we can take a look at JB on our way to town. If they've killed some of our outfit then we need to handle them.'

'Sure.' Hart nodded. 'Go along, ma'am. You're safe now. We'll be between you and anyone trying to come up with you.'

Hart put the reins back into the woman's hands and slapped the horse on the rump as he stepped back. The animal went forward again, and Mrs Baines cracked her whip and continued. Hart resumed his saddle and they went on at a fast clip. Hart thought of Pete O'Hara, recalling how the cowboy had been tied to the hitch rack in front of Crane's saloon, and anger surged through him.

Benteen headed off the trail and they swung north-east to approach the JB spread. The ranch house appeared before them and, as they approached at a gallop, a rifle cracked and a bullet whined over Hart's head.

He saw gunsmoke flare from the doorway of the barn and drew his Colt. Benteen motioned to a couple of the cowboys and rode off at an angle to approach the house from the rear. Hart settled himself lower in his saddle and continued straight into the yard, pistol raised, his keen gaze watching for resistance. He noted at least eight horses in the corral off to the left.

Four men came out of the house at a run. They were carrying weapons, and began shooting at the approaching riders. Hart triggered his pistol and the sound of shooting swelled. Two rifles opened fire from the open doorway of the barn, and Hart dismounted quickly when a slug bored through his leather holster. He emptied his pistol at the barn doorway and one of the guns fell silent.

Benteen and two men came around the left front corner or the house. Benteen paused at a window on the porch and peered into the big front room. He smashed a pane of glass with the muzzle of his pistol, and then thrust his hand through the hole and triggered the weapon. Gunsmoke drifted fast on the wind. A bullet from inside the house smashed an upper pane in the window and Benteen was showered with broken glass. He ducked below the sill and hastily reloaded his spent chambers.

Hart moved up on the right, attracting fire with every step, to which he replied with controlled ferocity. He gained the right side of the porch, reloaded his gun, and then stepped on to the porch and ran to the big front door. Benteen shouted something which Hart did not understand, and Hart paused, turning an enquiring gaze towards the A Bar M ranch foreman.

'I saw Bart Crane inside the house,' Benteen yelled. 'He's heavily bandaged.'

Hart frowned, wondering if he had heard Benteen correctly. Crane was supposed to be seriously wounded in Ashville. He moved back a couple of steps and then hurled himself at the door, which shook but did not give way. Someone inside the house fired two shots through the door, and Hart felt one of them clip his hat brim. He lunged at the door for a second time and burst the lock. The door flew inwards and Hart's momentum carried him across the threshold. He dropped flat as a gun blasted at him from the right, and felt the burn of a slug across his right shoulder blade. He rolled to the left and finished up on one knee, his pistol levelling at an indistinct figure across the smoke-filled room.

Hart fired and his adversary spun around and pitched to the floor. But the man was not finished. He rolled and pushed himself up into a kneeling position, his pistol lifting unsteadily, seeking a target. Hart recognized Bart Crane, and shifted his aim slightly as he fired at the saloon man. His slug thudded high into Crane's chest and the man pitched forward on to his face.

The shooting outside died away, and Hart pushed himself to his feet. Benteen appeared in the doorway, grinning. Gun echoes were fading slowly into the vast distance of the range.

'Looks like we've put them out if it,' Benteen said. 'What's Crane doing here? I thought you said you'd half-killed him.'

Hart approached the motionless Crane, who was lying on his face, and turned him over. Crane's eyes flickered open and he gazed up at Hart without registering recognition. Hart dropped to one knee beside the man. Crane was hit hard, but Hart thought he would survive.

'If Crane was well enough to ride out from town then he should have been put behind bars,' Hart said. 'The doc said he would take care of it. But there's no telling with a man like Crane. I'd better split the breeze to Ashville and see what has been going on.'

'The shooting here is over,' Benteen said. 'Two of my outfit have taken slugs, but they'll live. We'll ride in with you.'

'Get a wagon hitched, put the wounded in it, and come on to town. I'll ride ahead. Bascombe and his bunch should be in Ashville by now, and I don't want them getting away again.'

'I'll leave two of the crew to bring in the wounded – the rest of us will ride with you.' Benteen spoke harshly, and Hart did not argue.

They went out to the porch, and Hart was surprised to see snowflakes whirling across the yard. He stopped in mid-stride and looked around intently, and then sighed heavily and went to his horse. He swung into the saddle and galloped away from the ranch. The snow eased and then stopped, but an occasional flake drifted around him, and he was glad that the wind was blowing from behind.

Benteen came up alongside Hart and they rode together with two cowboys following closely behind. Hart considered the general situation, aware that if he could nail the outlaws then his job would be over. They maintained a mile-eating lope in a south-easterly direction, and almost three hours passed before the little township of Ashville rose up out of the undulating range.

'Those outlaws will be tough men to fight,' Benteen observed as they reached the street.

The livery barn was on the left, and Hart dismounted and led his horse inside. Nat Askew, the liveryman, emerged from his office, and he grinned at Hart.

'It's a good job you're here,' he said. 'There's big trouble in town. A gang of hardcases rode in about an hour ago; six of them. They stopped off at the law office and shot Walt Halfnight when he took a shotgun to them. Doc went into the office, but he ain't come out again. Three of the strangers went along to the saloon, and there's been some noise coming from there – tables being smashed, and glass. I heard tell they're the Bascombe gang. Their leader has a big scar on his face.'

'What happened with Bart Crane?' Hart enquired.

'I didn't see him after you shot him, but I heard he got the drop on the doc after he was patched up, and left town in a hurry. I reckon he's made a run for it.'

'He's on his way back again,' Hart said, 'with another bullet hole. Is Walt Halfnight dead?'

'I don't know. Like I said, after that shot in the law office, Doc went inside and ain't showed since.'

Benteen put their horses in a stall. Hart checked his pistol. He looked at the old ostler.

'You reckon there are three of the hardcases in the law office and another three in Crane's saloon, huh?'

154

'That's it.' Askew nodded eagerly. Apprehension was showing on his face. 'Is there gonna be shooting?'

'I don't know any other way of dealing with outlaws,' Hart said softly. 'What happened to Gedge? He was in jail when I left town.'

'I ain't heard a thing about him,' Askew replied.

Hart eased his pistol back into its holster and went out to the street. Benteen joined him, reloading his six-gun. Hart looked around the street, his gaze narrowed and calculating.

'I'll walk into the law office alone,' he decided. 'You can cover my back, Hemp. When the shooting starts, those outlaws in the saloon will come running.'

'OK. You don't have to worry about your back,' Benteen said grimly.

Hart set off along the sidewalk and made straight for the law office. The door was closed, and he saw a shadowed face peering out through the front window to the left of the door. He eased his gun in its holster, and then opened the door with his left hand and stepped inside. Three men were in the office. Two were lounging at the desk and one, whom Hart recognized as Taco Tate, was standing near the back wall, holding a rifle.

'This office is closed,' Tate rasped, lifting the muzzle of the rifle.

'Where is Bascombe?' Hart demanded.

The question threw Tate off guard and the muzzle of his rifle paused in its upward lift.

'Who in hell are you?' he demanded. 'What do you want with Bascombe?'

'I've got a message for him from Bart Crane.'

'Say, where is Crane? Bascombe has been looking all over for him. If he's trying to pull a fast one on the gang, Bascombe will shoot his eyes out.'

'So where is Bascombe?' Hart persisted.

'He went to the saloon, looking for Crane.' Tate began to lift the muzzle of his rifle again.

'You're Taco Tate, huh?' Hart readied himself for action. 'I've seen your face on a poster at Ranger Headquarters in San Antonio. Throw down that rifle and raise your hands. I'm a Texas Ranger. You're under arrest.'

Tate froze for a moment, his eyes widening in shock. Hart reached for his gun, and it came out fast and smoothly as Tate recovered and tried to get his rifle into action. Hart fired a shot that shook the office. Tate jerked under the impact of the slug and a splotch of blood appeared in the centre of his big chest. He twisted, dropped the rifle, and then followed it to the floor. His boot-heels beat a rapid tattoo of death on the boards.

Hart was already turning on the other two. Both men were shocked into immobility, and then they scrambled to their feet, reaching for their holstered guns. Benteen fired immediately from his position in the doorway, and the man on the left folded at the waist and jack-knifed to the floor. Hart triggered his smoking six-gun, aiming for a shoulder-shot on the second man, who was unable to complete his draw before hot lead smacked into him. He fell across the desk.

Gunsmoke drifted across the office as Hart looked around, his ears ringing from the crash of the shots. He picked up the bunch of keys lying on the desk and walked across to the door that led into the cells. Entering, he found Doc Chilvers in a cell, and unlocked the door. The doctor was grasping the bars of the door, his face showing impatience.

'Thank Heaven it's you!' he gasped. 'Where have you been? Murder was committed here. Walt Halfnight is dead.'

Hart stifled his regret and stepped back as Chilvers emerged from the cell. Hart looked around.

'Where's Gedge?' he demanded.

'I haven't seen him. You'll have to ask those gangsters in the office.'

'They're not in a fit condition to answer questions,' Hart replied.

Doc Chilvers hurried into the front office, and he was examining the outlaws by the time Hart caught up with him. Benteen was standing by the street door, peering along the sidewalk in the direction of the saloon.

'It's mighty quiet in Crane's place now,' Benteen remarked, 'and there's no sign of anyone on the street.'

'I'll liven things up in the saloon,' Hart promised, and left the office. He walked towards the saloon, his body tensed, his sharp gaze missing nothing along the street, which was deserted. A few snowflakes were whisking around, chivvied by the harsh wind; mere harbingers of future weather conditions, and he told himself that there was still time for him to finish this chore before the snow began to settle. He mentally counted the men he needed to face before he could be satisfied that the case was closed.

The sound of breaking glass sounded, and Benteen fired two quick shots from his position a couple of feet from Hart's left shoulder. Hart caught movement at an upper window of the saloon and flicked his gaze upwards to see a man's figure falling forward to pitch out of the window, a pistol falling from his right hand. The man thudded on the sidewalk in front of the batwings and lay motionless. Hart eased his pistol in its holster and strode to the swing doors.

He paused beside the doors, flattening against the wall, gun in hand, and had no recollection of having drawn the weapon. He threw a glance at the dead man on the sidewalk and exhaled sharply when he recognized Pat Gedge. The silence was intense, over-powering. Hart drew a deep breath, held it for a moment, and then called in an echoing tone.

'Bascombe, I'm Mike Hart; Texas Ranger. I've been hunting you. The place is surrounded, so come on out with your hands up.'

'If you want me then come in and get me,' a harsh voice replied from inside the saloon. 'I remember you, Hart, so come on and get what you've been asking for.'

Hart looked back at Benteen, who was flattened

158

against the front wall of the saloon beside a window. He made a motion with his left hand, indicating that Benteen should break the window and throw some lead inside. Benteen nodded and raised his pistol. Hart faced his front. He heard glass shattering and, when Benteen fired into the saloon, shouldered his way through the swing doors and lunged to the floor, his right hand lifting and angling his pistol at the big figure of Trace Bascombe. The outlaw, distracted by the broken window, was half-turned in that direction.

Bascombe recovered, crouching as he turned to face the threat that Hart posed. Hart fired as his muzzle lined up on the outlaw's belt buckle. He triggered two swift shots as Bascombe opened fire, but the gang leader was too slow. Hart's bullets struck him dead centre, and Bascombe's gun arm was already falling away as his first shot left the muzzle to bore into the sawdust three inches from Hart's left hand.

Bascombe fell to his knees, trying desperately to control his pistol. His face was contorted, his eyes blazing with hatred and frustration. Then he slackened and his hand fell away. He pitched forward on to his face and slumped into death.

Hart turned in time to see Benteen nail the third outlaw. He regained his feet but the action was over, echoes fading slowly. The ensuing silence seemed harder to take than the raucous thunder that had blasted through the saloon with the power of an avenging angel. Benteen was reloading his pistol. He looked up at Hart and nodded.

'Looks like you got it done,' he commented.

Hart nodded and walked out to the street. It was done for all those men who had plotted, schemed and murdered for crooked gains, but it was never over for him. He was following a trail that only death could end. He stopped in the street and looked around. Folk were emerging from the buildings now, as if scenting that the trouble was over. He looked up into the grey sky, and the icy wind scoured his face. A snow flake settled on his nose. He exhaled slowly, ridding himself of tension, and all the other emotions that lurked inside.

It was time to send a wire to Captain Buckbee.